A HERCULEAH JONES MYSTERY

KING OF MURDER

BY BETSY BYARS

SLEUTH
PUFFIN

PUFFIN BOOKS

Published by the Penguin Group

Penguin Group (USA) Inc., 345 Hudson Street, New York, New York 10014, U.S.A.

Penguin Group (Canada), 90 Eglinton Avenue East, Suite 700, Toronto, Ontario, Canada M4P 2Y3
(a division of Pearson Penguin Canada Inc.)

Penguin Books Ltd, 80 Strand, London WC2R 0RL, England

Penguin Ireland, 25 St Stephen's Green, Dublin 2, Ireland
(a division of Penguin Books Ltd)

Penguin Group (Australia), 250 Camberwell Road, Camberwell, Victoria 3124, Australia
(a division of Pearson Australia Group Pty Ltd)

Penguin Books India Pvt Ltd, 11 Community Centre, Panchsheel Park, New Delhi - 110 017, India

Penguin Group (NZ), Cnr Airborne and Rosedale Roads, Albany, Auckland 1310, New Zealand
(a division of Pearson New Zealand Ltd)

Penguin Books (South Africa) (Pty) Ltd, 24 Sturdee Avenue,
Rosebank, Johannesburg 2196, South Africa

Registered Offices: Penguin Books Ltd, 80 Strand, London WC2R 0RL, England

First published in the United States of America by Viking,
a division of Penguin Young Readers Group, 2006
This Sleuth edition published by Puffin Books,
a division of Penguin Young Readers Group, 2007

1 3 5 7 9 10 8 6 4 2

Copyright © Betsy Byars, 2006
All rights reserved

THE LIBRARY OF CONGRESS HAS CATALOGED THE VIKING EDITION AS FOLLOWS:

Byars, Betsy Cromer.
King of Murder / by Betsy Byars.
p.   cm.—(A Herculeah Jones mystery)
Summary: Herculeah meets a murder mystery writer, and has the uneasy feeling
that he knows more about murder than he should.
ISBN 0-670-06065-8 (hardcover : alk. paper)
[1. Murder—Fiction. 2. Mystery and detective stories.] I. Title.
PZ7.B9836Kin 2006   [Fic]—dc22   2005008422

Puffin Books ISBN 978-0-14240759-2

Printed in the United States of America

Set in Minion
Book design by Sam Kim

A HERCULEAH JONES MYSTERY

KING OF MURDER

CONTENTS

A HERCULEAH JONES MYSTERY

KING OF MURDER

THE DEATH NOTE

"Don't go in there!"

Meat and Herculeah were in front of Hidden Treasures, the secondhand store where Herculeah liked to shop. Her hand was reaching for the doorknob, but at Meat's warning, she paused.

"Why not?"

Meat noticed that her fingers curled around the knob. She never listened to him, but this was important. He had to try.

"Because every time you get something in there, it leads to murder," he said.

"It does not."

"How about that coat you bought in there with the note from a dead woman in the pocket? The 'I don't want to die; he's going to kill me' note."

"May I remind you," Herculeah said, "that I also bought the camera in here that let us find your father."

"Well, yes."

"I also got those granny glasses that make me think better. And my binocs! I would have missed a lot without my binoculars. I've gotten lots of good stuff here. I'm going in."

"Fine. Go in. Just don't buy anything. That's when the trouble starts."

"I can't buy anything. I don't have any money. You?"

"No."

"Then nothing can happen to us. We're safe."

"I don't know how and I don't know why and don't ask me to explain it, but I know we'll have found something that will lead to murder."

Herculeah opened the door. "You coming?"

"What do you think?"

"I think you're going to hesitate and make me think you aren't going to come in, and then you're going to come in."

He sighed. He wished just once he could surprise Herculeah and do the unexpected, but this was not the time. He hesitated and then followed her inside.

Later, when Meat looked back on his prediction, he realized he should have added two words. The prediction should have been, "I don't know how and I don't know why and don't ask me to explain it, but we'll have found something *or someone* that will lead to murder."

2

A MAN IN BLACK

Herculeah breezed into the shop. Behind her, Meat came in more slowly and closed the door behind him.

"Hi, Mrs. Jay, it's me."

"Oh, Herculeah! Come in!"

"Neither of us has any money, Mrs. Jay; we just want to look around."

Over the years, Herculeah and Mrs. Jay had become friends, and Mrs. Jay smiled warmly at Herculeah. "I'm glad it's you, because I've got someone I especially want you to meet."

Herculeah walked to the back of the shop where Mrs. Jay stood with a tall man. He was dressed all in black, and his sharp eyes beneath the brim of his black hat were black, too.

As she got closer, she noticed that he wore a cape. Herculeah hadn't ever seen a man in a cape, outside of a Dracula movie.

"Herculeah, this is the man I told you about. He writes murder mysteries." To the man she said, "Herculeah loves mysteries. She's even solved quite a few."

"You're a writer?" Herculeah asked. Perhaps that explained the cape. Her face was bright with interest.

"Wonderful murder mysteries," Mrs. Jay said. "People tell me his murders are so realistic, you almost feel like you're there, committing them yourself."

"Mrs. Jay is too kind," the man said.

"Well, I know a good murder mystery when I hear about it. I don't read much. I don't have time."

He took off his hat in an old-timey gesture. "Mathias King, at your service."

"Mathias King!" Herculeah exclaimed. "Mrs. Jay, you did tell me about him. I remember now. And, and"—Herculeah's excitement grew—"you told me some of the fake murder weapons that inspired his books were bought right here in this very store. I even read *A Slash of Life*!"

"That's right," Mrs. Jay said. "He's written—I don't know how many books—and all the murder weapons came from Hidden Treasures."

"All of them?" Herculeah asked.

"Just my last two," Mathias King admitted. "My other books were true-crime books—nonfiction. You might have heard of some of them—*The Case of the Murdered Monk* was perhaps my most famous."

Herculeah still looked interested, but it was obvious that she hadn't heard of the unfortunate monk.

Mathias King continued quickly. "However, it was not until

I began selecting my weapons here and creating my own murders that I became"—he shrugged as if he hated to say the word, but he had to because it was true—"famous."

"The first weapon you bought from me," Mrs. Jay said with a smile of remembrance, "was the letter opener."

"Ah, that was featured in *A Slash of Life*," Mathias King said. "But it was no ordinary letter opener. Oh, no, it was like a very lovely stiletto." His long, thin fingers drew out the blade in the air, and then with a quick jab thrust it into a victim.

"And the second one was the cup."

"Ah, yes, the cup, but I like to think of it as a goblet. The goblet was featured in *A Sip of Death*. But it was no ordinary vessel. It was from the old days. I even like to think that it had once belonged to the Marchese of Rome."

"If it belonged to him, you owe me a bunch of money," Mrs. Jay laughed.

"The bowl of the goblet was an apple." His hand cupped the invisible fruit. "And twining up the stem was a snake." Now the fingers became a snake, coiling around the stem of the goblet. "The snake's head contained just the tiniest little amount of poison. A touch on the handle of the goblet, and the snake's mouth opened, his forked tongue appeared, and on the tongue—*voilà*—a drop of venom."

"I don't remember any snake," Mrs. Jay said.

Mathias King smiled. "That's why you let me have it so

cheaply." Then, still smiling, he lifted his eyes from the invisible apple and saw Meat.

Meat was standing a counter away, keeping his distance.

"The young man is with you?" Mathias King said.

"Yes, that's my friend Meat."

"Welcome to the conversation, Meat. Mathias King, at your service."

"My name's Albert," Meat said. He was particular about who called him Meat.

"Allllbert," Mathias King said, drawing out the Ls in a way that made Meat sorry that the man knew any of his names.

Mathias King gave a shrug. It was a practiced move that tossed his cape back over one shoulder.

"Even though you know my name, I'd like you to still think of me as a man of mystery. Everyone does. They glance at me on the street as I pass. They wonder about me behind my back."

No wonder, Meat thought.

He gave Meat a smile that revealed pointed teeth. Meat felt as if Mathias King had read his mind.

Herculeah hadn't seen teeth like that outside of—once again—a Dracula movie.

"And sometimes," he continued, "they even buy my books."

"Oh, they all buy your books." Mrs. Jay spoke quickly, feeling she had been out of the conversation long enough. She held up a black bag that had been on the counter.

"This is his shopping bag, only he calls it his Murder Bag."

3

THE GOLDEN WHATEVER

"Murder Bag?" Herculeah said.

"It holds his weapons," Mrs. Jay said. "And they tell me that he also has a murder room in his house, though I've never seen it."

"Now you're giving away all my secrets," Mathias King said.

"And he never lets anyone inside his Den of Iniquity—that's what he calls it—not even the housekeeper."

"Oh, I might make an exception every now and then," he said, smiling at Herculeah.

Herculeah wasn't sure she wanted to go near anything called a den of iniquity. Iniquity, she knew, meant wickedness.

She changed the subject. "And is the weapon for your next book in your Murder Bag, Mr. King?" Herculeah asked.

Mrs. Jay said, "No, he bought that last week. It's the golden—"

Mathias King stopped her with a gesture. "Give them no clue. They will have to read the book."

"—the golden whatever," Mrs. Jay finished lamely. Behind

his back, she indicated something the size of a small bed.

"That's just one possibility, Mrs. Jay. I always keep an open mind where my murder weapon is concerned. And these young people may have fresh ideas. Let's take a look, shall we?"

He began to move through the aisle, his long hands fluttering over the items—a Statue of Liberty bank, a globe, a cigarette lighter in the shape of a pistol. He hesitated over the cigarette lighter and then picked up an Oriental box and slid off the top. "Empty." He showed it to Herculeah.

"But this could be a trick box, and when you open it a snake comes out and strikes."

He passed his fingers over the box and placed it in her hand. She slid open the top. A cloth snake sprang out and touched her throat. She was startled, but she didn't flinch.

"But you've already used a snake," Herculeah said quickly, handing him the snake and the box. "You wouldn't want to repeat yourself."

"Ah, yes, I must not repeat myself."

Mrs. Jay said, "Mathias was once a magician, so he can make you believe anything."

"Now, Mrs. Jay, once again you are too kind."

He moved through the tables, picking up an object here, another there.

"Ah, here's something. What is this meant to be, Mrs. Jay?"

"It holds back draperies. It's a silken rope."

Mathias King picked it up and let it slip through his fingers.

"I like this. It has a deadly feel to it. And the silk appeals to me. I am drawn to beautiful weapons."

He did a trick with the rope so that it seemed to stand up all by itself for a moment, and then coiled it gracefully into one hand.

He moved backward, as if to give himself more room. His hands moved so quickly, so skillfully, that the three of them watched, as fascinated as if they were at a real magic show.

"It could be used to tie a victim's hands." He bound his own wrists so that he seemed to be caught in the golden rope.

"But a skillful victim might break free. Or, let me see, the rope could be a noose—"

And as he spoke, he swirled and tossed the rope over Meat's head and drew it back against his throat.

The movement was so quick that Meat had no time to react. And, just as quickly, the golden rope slid across Meat's throat and disappeared into the folds of Mathias King's cape.

The rope had barely brushed Meat's throat, and yet it left him unable to swallow. He knew if he tried, his throat would protest with a loud unpleasant *glunk*, and everyone would know he had been afraid.

He turned away as if bored—at least that was how he hoped he looked—and moved back out of the way. He was so upset, he was relieved to be able to locate the door. He started for it.

"Wait. Wait!" Mathias King called after him. "Oh, I mean no harm. Please, wait." Mathias King's voice had softened with remorse. "Come back."

Herculeah could see from the set of Meat's shoulders that coming back was not an option. "We'd better go," she said. Her throat felt sort of tight, too.

"But I meant no harm. It was just a trick. Oh, dear, Mrs. Jay. I have run off your customers."

"We didn't have any money," Herculeah admitted.

"At least take the box as a memento of the visit. Mrs. Jay, put this on my account."

He held out the Oriental box to her, but she shook her head. "No, thanks." She could still feel the unpleasant tap of the trick snake against her throat.

"Well, will you at least take my card?"

Herculeah paused.

Mr. King reached into a pocket and brought out a packet of cards.

"I have many cards because I have been many things." He began to shuffle through the cards. "Let's see. 'Mathias King, King of Magicians' . . . 'Mathias King, King of Actors' . . . Ah, here is the one I want you to have."

Herculeah took the card and read the inscription.

Mathias King
KING OF MURDER

4

EITHER...OR

"Did you see that? Did you see that?"

"What?"

"He tried to strangle me!"

Herculeah and Meat were now outside Hidden Treasures, on their way home. Meat had stopped Herculeah as soon as they were away from the window and out of sight of Mrs. Jay and, more importantly, Mr. Mathias King.

"He didn't try to strangle you. He was just kidding. I could tell from the expression on his face that he was putting on an act for Mrs. Jay and me."

"You call that kidding? Putting a rope around someone's neck and choking them?"

"It wasn't a rope and it wasn't that tight, Meat. And it was only, like, two seconds and the cord disappeared. I never did see where it went, did you?"

"It felt tight." He walked slower. "I've never told you this, but fear sort of causes my throat to close up. Even now I can't swallow without making a sound like this—*glunk*."

Herculeah said, "Oh?" as if she wasn't aware of the affliction. She had actually heard that *glunk* many times.

"My throat tends to tighten up, too," she said. "Everybody's does, but Mathias King was just . . . Oh, I don't know." She shrugged. "He's a writer, Meat. Writers are weird."

"He's weird, all right; I agree with that. But not all writers are weird," Meat said.

"I didn't know you knew any writers." She looked at him, as if studying his truthfulness.

"One or two."

"You never told me you knew any writers."

"You never asked."

"I'm asking now. Name one."

"You don't believe I know writers?" Meat said, his mind racing for a literary name. To his great relief, he got one. "Elizabeth Ann Varner?"

"Who's she?"

He smiled, remembering. "She was a very nice author who came to my first-grade class."

"That was the year you were in Miss Stroupe's room, and I was stuck with Deviled Egg. So what kind of books did Elizabeth Ann Varner write?"

"Funny ones."

"Go on. I could use a laugh."

"She had a series about two donkeys."

"Donkeys?"

"Yes," Meat said, warming to his story. "Their names were Hee and Haw, and Hee had a louder hee-haw than Haw, and that's how they told them apart, but one day Haw's hee-haw—"

He saw the way Herculeah was looking at him, and he said quickly, "Oh, never mind."

"No, you've got me interested. Did Haw ever get as loud a hee-haw as Hee or—"

"I said never mind!"

He could tell from her voice that she was amused. First she had belittled his getting strangled—calling it kidding and an act—and now she was belittling Hee and Haw, two of his favorite characters in the world. One of the books about Hee and Haw was the first book he had read by himself, and he read it well, too. Even his mom had described his hee-haws as forceful.

They walked to the corner in silence, then Herculeah said, "Getting back to our original topic . . ."

"Please," Meat said.

"Authors—some authors," she corrected herself, "are a little weird. They have to be. They sit in front of their computers all day and write about life instead of going out and experiencing it.

"And," she went on as they crossed the street, "mystery writers are perhaps a little weirder than the others."

"Why? Because they sit in front of their computers writing about murder instead of going out and doing it?"

Herculeah stopped. She thought for a minute and then said, "You've got a point, Meat."

"I do? What?"

"Well, when I saw Mr. King with the golden noose, as he called it, he really seemed like a different person. And when he threw it over your head, well, I thought, wow, this is a writer who really knows his characters—this is a writer who gets inside his characters' minds."

She took in a deep breath. He could tell she had something to add, and Herculeah's additions were usually important.

"Go on."

"Either he really does get inside his characters' minds or—"

"Or what?"

"Or he's a murderer."

5

THE VICTIM

Mathias King stood at the window of Hidden Treasures. He watched Herculeah and Meat until they were out of sight.

"Interesting girl," he commented, more to himself than to Mrs. Jay, but she answered.

"Oh, yes, Herculeah is an interesting girl. She's been a customer for a long time. You and she have very different goals."

"Oh?"

"She buys items that will help her discover murders, and you get items to help your characters commit them."

He was only half listening and appeared lost in thought.

"She would make a fascinating victim," he said.

Mrs. Jay took a step backward. "You're thinking of putting Herculeah in one of your books?"

"It's just a thought. At first," he went on, "I was thinking of the young man. He had the feel of a victim, wouldn't you agree? Certainly he's placid, wouldn't put up much of a struggle..."

"I don't know him that well."

Mathias King turned away from the window to face Mrs. Jay. "Did you see how he froze when I tightened the noose around his neck?"

"Yes, you scared him."

"I could have tightened the noose and strangled him if I'd wanted to—if, of course," he laughed, "I were a real murderer."

"I guess so."

"And then," he went on, his voice rising with his enthusiasm, "did you notice Herculeah's reaction when I did the snake bit with the Oriental box?"

"Her back was to me. I didn't see."

"She didn't like it, but she looked straight at me with those gray eyes that . . . Could you see her eyes, Mrs. Jay?"

"No."

"When you first introduced us and I noticed her extraordinary gray eyes, I was struck with their warmth—the soft gray of a kitten, of an evening sky—"

"My, you're becoming poetic, Mathias."

"You've discovered another of my talents, Mrs. Jay, but you didn't let me finish." He struck a pose so that his tall, thin frame seemed to be spotlit. "The soft veiled curtain of an evening sky that falls on a weary world."

"Even more poetic."

"You're too kind."

"Yes, I guess I am."

"But when I did the trick with the Oriental box, her eyes changed. They became the hard, clear silver of bayonet steel."

"I'm sorry I missed that."

"Remember what she said to me?"

"Not word for word."

"I think you're having fun at my expense, Mrs. Jay, but that's all right. She said, as cool as ice, 'But you've already used a snake. You wouldn't want to repeat yourself,' which of course I had."

He shook his head as if abandoning the spotlight. "She would not be an easy victim. I sometimes think my victims are too easy."

"No, she wouldn't be an easy victim. Plus the fact that her mother is a private investigator and her father is a police lieutenant."

He smiled his commanding smile, showing his pointed teeth. "Yes," he said, "that would make it challenging."

THE THINK COCOON

"Beware! Beware!"

"I hear your parrot in the background," Meat said. "He must be upset about something."

"He's always upset about something. He's been yelling, 'Beware' ever since I got home. And guess what else he's started doing?"

"I can't."

"He's learned to make the exact sound of a telephone ringing. That's why I called you. I heard the phone ringing, and when I picked it up, I heard the dial tone. So I knew it was Tarot. Anyway, I already had the phone in my hand so I called you."

"Well, I'm glad you did." A might-as-well call, he imagined, was better than no call.

"Me, too, because I was sitting here with my granny glasses on, trying to think, when all of a sudden it worked. I did think of something."

"What?"

"I was thinking about Mathias King and his books. And I realized we need to get copies of those books and read them more carefully and see if they were real murders."

"That sounds reasonable."

"One was *A Slash of Life*, and what was the other one?"

"*A Sip of Death*? That was about the apple and snake goblet."

"Yes! So tomorrow afternoon we'll go to your uncle Neiman's used-book store."

"Death's Door?" Meat asked, stalling for time.

"He hasn't changed the name?"

"No."

"I thought maybe with all the trouble he might have."

"It was named by his customers. They voted. The choices were Little Shop of Horrors, Murder for Sale, or Death's Door. Anyway, I can't go tomorrow. I have to go to the d-dentist."

Herculeah knew that Meat always stuttered when he was lying, but then having to go to the dentist could make one stutter as well.

"I didn't know the dentist was open on Saturday afternoon."

"Just for t-toothaches."

"Oh, I hate to have those." She sighed. "I always have more fun when you're along."

"Yeah, it must have been a lot of fun this afternoon to watch me get strangled." Maybe, he thought, it would have been better if he *had* been strangled. Then he wouldn't have to do what he had to do tomorrow.

"Actually, Meat, it happened so fast I hardly saw it." She paused. "It makes you realize . . . I mean, Meat, the man was once a magician. He could kill someone before they knew what was happening."

"Yeah, you're lying there dead going, Well, now I know what happened. Some consolation."

"You're not in a very good mood tonight."

Meat thought that was putting it mildly. He remembered that it was only this afternoon, when they were entering Hidden Treasures, that he had wished—just once—he could surprise Herculeah. Well, he was getting his wish, and like in those old fairy tales, you got your wish and lost everything.

"I'd better let you go. I'll try to get the books tomorrow. Which one do you want to read—*A Slash of Life* or *A Sip of Death*?"

"You choose."

"I'll let you know."

Tarot had been ignored for too long. He'd had a brief moment of satisfaction when he rang like the telephone and Herculeah answered it, but that didn't last long.

"Ring!"

"Did you hear that, Meat? That was Tarot doing his telephone imitation."

"I heard it."

"Hel-lo!"

"Did you hear that? Now he's answering himself."

Tarot gave up on the telephone and called, "Beware! Beware!"

"You know what worries me about that parrot and all his bewares?" Meat said.

"What?"

"Sometimes Tarot knows what he's talking about."

AT DEATH'S DOOR

Herculeah stood in front of Death's Door. She hesitated, because going through her mind was that awful night when she had almost been the Bull's victim there.

She remembered the Bull had leaned down and peered through the books at her. His terrible hooded eyes had looked directly at her. His eyes were red and seemed to be lit from within like something at Halloween.

"You," he had said.

He had exhaled, and Herculeah had smelled the fetid breath of death.

Well, the Bull was long gone. She shook herself, took a deep breath, and opened the door.

"Back here," Uncle Neiman called.

She moved to the back of the store where Uncle Neiman waited behind his desk. He looked up at her through his thick glasses.

"It's me, Herculeah Jones," she said.

"Oh, Herculeah, Herculeah. You saved my life that terrible night. You can have anything in the store—take as many books as you like."

"Actually, I do want some books—but just two of them. I hope you have them."

"If it's about murder or suspense or mayhem or mystery, I've got them."

"It is. I met a man named Mathias King—"

"Ah, the King of Murder," Uncle Neiman said. "You want *A Slash of Life* and *A Sip of Death*."

"You know Mathias King?"

"Everybody knows Mathias King. He's had signings in this very shop."

"People came and bought his books and he autographed them?"

"Oh, yes, he has a good local following. At the last signing there must have been fifty people in here. They brought in a busload of folks from Magnolia Downs."

"Magnolia Downs?"

"The retirement center out on Peachford Road. He gave a brief talk and did tricks while he was talking—he's very amusing. I couldn't catch all the tricks because of my eyesight, but the audience did. There were a lot of ohs and ahs."

"He was a magician before he became a writer, right?"

"Among other things."

Uncle Neiman got up from his desk and began to move through the stacks. He moved with such precision that Herculeah realized bad eyesight didn't matter here. He knew his books.

"Ah," he said as he ran his fingers over the spines of the books and pulled out a title. "I only have one," he said in a disappointed way. "These books are very popular."

He looked at the cover for a moment and then presented the book to her. "With my compliments," he said.

"But let me pay for it. For once, I've got money."

"The book is a gift."

"Thank you."

She glanced at the cover. There was a picture of a woman with a knife protruding from her back and a lot of blood on what appeared to be a nightgown. Her red lips, parted in a grimace, and the blood on her nightgown dominated the picture.

On the back cover was a picture of Mathias King in his black cape and hat. The blurb about the book began, "Her lips tried to form the name of her killer but . . ."

Uncle Neiman interrupted her reading. "Come, Herculeah, sit with me for a moment. I just remembered something that might interest you about Mathias King."

"Everything about Mathias King interests me."

They moved back to his desk. Uncle Neiman took his usual place in the swivel chair, and Herculeah perched on the edge of the desk. She leaned toward him. She didn't want to miss a word.

"There was a woman here that day—she was from Magnolia Downs. Mathias took questions after his speech and they were very ordinary questions—'Where do you get your ideas?' 'What's your next book going to be about?' And then this woman stood up, and even with my poor eyesight I sensed that her question was going to be different."

"And was it?"

"Oh, yes. She said she had a friend who died the same way that the woman in *A Slash of Life* did, and she wondered if he had known the woman."

"Did she give the friend's name?"

"I don't believe she did, but I got the feeling that Mathias King didn't need the name."

"Did Mathias King seem upset about the question?"

"I don't think he was happy about it. But he shrugged it off and said he might have read something about it in the paper. Sometimes he did get ideas from real murders."

"Or," Herculeah said, "from murders he committed."

Uncle Neiman looked at her. His pale eyes, large behind the thick glasses, seemed to sharpen.

"I never thought of that before, but I suppose it's possible," he said.

8

RETURN TO THE DARK AGES

Meat stood at the front window of his house even though there was nothing to see. His shoulders were slumped. His hands were jammed into his pockets.

Herculeah had long ago departed for Death's Door. She had come out of her house in her usual rush. She had turned in the direction of town, a sweater tied around her waist, her hair flying out behind her like a cape. Superwoman.

He had hoped she might glance across the street, see him, and give him a wave of sympathy for his upcoming dental visit. But, no, as if she already knew he didn't deserve any sympathy, she hurried on down the sidewalk and turned the corner.

He knew his mother had come into the room from the kitchen, because he smelled mayonnaise. "You want a sandwich?"

Of course he wanted a sandwich, he had never not wanted a sandwich in his whole life, but he shook his head. "I'm not feeling well," he said. "I may be coming down with something."

"Don't bother trying that I'm-coming-down-with-something trick." His mother's tone made it a warning. She crossed the room and put her hand on his forehead.

"I know I don't have any fever," he snapped.

He wished, as he had many times, that there was some simple way to get a few degrees of fever when you were desperate to get out of something. He knew from past experience that there wasn't.

"Get your jacket."

He went to the hall closet and came back dragging an athletic sweatshirt that had seen better days.

"I said a jacket, not a rag." Another warning.

Meat went back to the closet. When he returned to the room, he said, "I still can't believe you're doing this terrible thing to me."

"Terrible thing? What terrible thing? Taking a beautiful young girl for pizza and a movie is a terrible thing?"

"It's a terrible thing to make arrangements behind your children's back. It's like a return to the Dark Ages."

"In some respects the Dark Ages weren't so bad." She took a deep breath. "Anyway, I owe my friend Dottie big-time. When your father deserted us—and there's no other word to describe what he did—it was my friend Dottie who kept me from falling apart. You think it's easy to be deserted by a husband?"

"No, but—"

"Dottie listened to my fears—and I had plenty of those. She dried my tears—I had plenty of those, too. She cooked meals for us. She slept over when I needed her. She was better than a psychiatrist. When I see psychiatrists on TV, I think to myself, You're pretty good, but you're no Dottie."

She paused to get her breath. She was getting kind of red in the face—a color that was not becoming on her—so Meat said, "All right, all right, I get the message."

That didn't stop his mother. "And in all those years since your father deserted us, did she ever ask a favor of me?"

"I guess not."

"Now, she asks one tiny favor. Her niece Steffie is visiting and she wants to arrange an outing. She thinks of you, Albert. You think I could say no?"

"Obviously not," Meat said.

"Don't try to be smart."

"I'm not trying to be smart, Mom. I'm just trying to stay alive in the Dark Ages."

"You mark my words. When you get home this afternoon, you'll thank me for a wonderful afternoon."

It seemed unlikely, but Meat said, "I hope so."

9

QUESTIONS WITHOUT ANSWERS

Uncle Neiman and Herculeah were silent for a moment, thinking about what had just been said. Their comments lay heavily between them, yet neither one took back their statement.

"What else did the woman say?" Herculeah prompted.

"I'm trying to remember her exact words, but she was at the back of the room. I do remember that she said the police had ruled her friend's death a homicide, and that the murder weapon—a knife—was never found. Ever since she had read *A Slash of Life*, she had wondered if he knew anything about that. It was almost as if she was accusing him of having the knife.

"Mathias King said, 'In my book, the knife was found in the victim's back, not her chest.'

"'I don't believe I mentioned that my friend was stabbed in the chest. How did you know that?' the woman said.

"'Thank you for your interest and questions,' he said firmly.

It was as if he'd closed the door on further questions, but she was determined to push it open.

"The woman went on to say that all the details of the house in the book were exactly the things in her friend's house—even a large jade Buddha in the front hallway. She said she didn't know how he could have gotten those exact details unless he had been there. 'Were you ever in my friend's house?' She asked that point-blank. Then she added, 'She lived on—' and gave the name of the street—it was Hawthorn or Oak or some tree."

"Did he answer?"

"No, and after that he didn't take any more questions—just turned to me and said, 'Isn't this supposed to be a signing?' And he leaned forward and pulled a fountain pen from behind a woman's ear.

"Later, after the audience had left, he came up to me and asked who the inquisitive woman was. I told him."

"And what did he say?"

"I remember his exact words: 'Hmmmm. Interesting.'"

Herculeah listened intently. "Do you still remember the woman's name who asked the questions?"

"Oh, yes. I met her before the signing. I remember her name because she had the same name as one of my favorite movie stars—Rita Hayworth. She said all her friends at the Downs call her Gilda—that was Hayworth's best role."

"Rita Hayworth, and she lives at Magnolia Downs. Where is that exactly?"

"Take the Eastmont bus. It stops right at Peachford Street."

"Well, this has really been helpful," Herculeah said. "Not only did I get the book, but I got a lead to a mystery I'm trying to solve."

The bell above the door jangled as a customer entered the shop, and Herculeah said, "Oh, you've got another customer. Don't let me take up all of your time."

"They can wait."

"I'm sorry that Meat—I mean, your nephew Albert—couldn't come with me. He had a dental appointment."

"I thought Sears said he was going on a—" He broke off as a customer came around the stacks.

Herculeah was so shocked at hearing the word "Sears" that she didn't take in what Uncle Neiman had said.

Herculeah knew that Meat's mom and her sisters and brothers had all been named for stores. Uncle Neiman had been named for Neiman Marcus, and there was a Tiffany and a Macy.

Herculeah had been fascinated. She'd known people named for states, even cities, but stores?

She had found out, after begging Meat, that his mother's name was Sears. Meat had told her to never, ever mention this because nobody was supposed to know, and his mother would be terribly upset if anyone ever, ever called her Sears.

She couldn't believe that Uncle Neiman had said the forbidden word.

"I didn't think anybody was supposed to say her name," she said.

"I'm her brother. I've been saying her name all my life." He smiled at her. "But you'd better not say it."

"Oh, I won't."

The customer, empty-handed, waited until their conversation was over. Then she said, "You don't have one single Mathias King book."

"She just got the last one," Uncle Neiman said.

Herculeah smiled and said, "Sorry."

"What'd you get?"

Herculeah held up the book.

"Oh, *A Slash of Life*. I've read that two times. It's scary."

"I've read it, too, and it is scary, but so is the man who wrote it."

The woman laughed. "You must have met Mathias King. Well, I guess I'll have to look for something else."

More people were entering the shop, so Herculeah said, "I'd better be going. Good-bye, and thanks again for the book."

"You are more than welcome."

Herculeah was already out the door when she wondered what the last half of Uncle Neiman's sentence would have been. "I thought Sears said he was going on a—"

Oh, well, sooner or later she would find out the answer to that question. Now she had to get to Magnolia Downs and find the answer to murder.

PUSHING UP THE SKY

"I'm looking for a Miss Rita Hayworth," Herculeah told the woman at the desk.

Magnolia Downs had a big airy front parlor. It looked more like a Southern mansion than a place for retired people. Herculeah realized she didn't know any retired people—the older people she knew in her neighborhood ran businesses out of their homes—Cakes by Cheri; One-Hour Dentals; her mother's Mim Jones, Private Investigator.

Well, maybe Meat's mother, Sears, could be considered retired. Anyway, Sears didn't work. Herculeah took a deep breath. I've got to stop thinking of her as Sears or I'll slip and call her that, she told herself.

The woman said, "I believe she just went to her Tai Chi class. That's in the sun room—past the dining room and to your right."

Herculeah walked down the hall and peered into the sun room. The class of men and women were lined up in two rows.

"Were you looking for someone?" the teacher asked. She was a short, cheerful woman. Her white hair looked like one of those bowl haircuts Herculeah had read about from the old days. Moms would cut their kids' hair by putting a bowl on the kid's head and cutting around it.

"Yes, but it can wait," Herculeah said. "I don't want to disturb the class."

"Well, join us. Are you familiar with Tai Chi?"

"No, but I'll try anything."

"I like that attitude."

Herculeah walked to the back of the class. She slipped off her backpack and dropped it to the floor.

"We'll warm up with the move known as the Wind in the Willows."

Everyone began swinging their arms, and Herculeah did, too. Tai Chi wasn't as hard as she thought it was going to be. She had envisioned people kicking at each other. She didn't especially want to be kicked—even by an elderly person.

"The energy originates in your feet, issues through your waist, and expresses itself in your arms."

As Herculeah swung her arms, she looked around at the members of the Tai Chi class, trying to figure out which one was Rita Hayworth. She settled on the tall, thin woman in the front row who looked like energy was really expressing itself in her arms. Herculeah could imagine that woman standing up in Death's Door and confronting Mathias King.

"Our next warm-up move is Pushing Up the Sky. Inhale when your hand pushes up; exhale when it comes down."

Herculeah wished Meat were here to push up the sky with her, but he was still at the dentist's office. She'd tried to call him after she left Death's Door.

Before she had the sky as high as she wanted it, Herculeah found herself doing the Turtle, then the Elephant Raises His Trunk. Then on to Gathering and Storing, and Sun and Moon Hands. There was no end to the different ways you could move your body.

When the class was over, Herculeah asked the woman beside her, "Is Rita Hayworth here today?"

"Oh, yes, she's always here."

"Is that her on the end of the front row?"

"No, Rita Hayworth is our teacher. Gilda, this young lady is looking for you."

The teacher came over. "I really enjoyed your class," Herculeah said. "Thanks for letting me join you."

"You're most welcome."

"I wasn't too good on Crane Opening His Wings, but I remember Gathering and Storing and I'm going to do that at home."

"It's one of our most important moves. Remember to let your feet claw the earth. You want to feel rooted—like a giant tree." She made clawing motions with her hands.

"I actually did feel sort of treelike." Herculeah smiled. "Course I'm so tall, I often feel treelike."

Rita Hayworth looked at her with bright eyes. "So, who are you and why did you want to see me?"

"I should have introduced myself. I'm Herculeah Jones."

"What a lovely name. I've never heard it before. Is it a family name?"

"Not really. My mom doesn't like me to tell this, but she was watching a Hercules movie in the hospital while she was waiting for me to be born. After she went in the delivery room, Mom was kidding around about naming me Hercules if I was a boy. And the nurse asked what she was going to name me if I was a girl, and out of the clear blue Mom said, 'If it's a girl, I'll name her Herculeah.' They were having fun with it and the doctor said, 'How about Samson? I've never delivered a Samson before.' He broke into a Russian song, 'Oh, Samson-ya.' Then when I was born and I was such a big strong baby, Herculeah seemed just right."

"It's a very beautiful name. And what can I do for you, Herculeah?" She gave the name such a beautiful pronunciation that it made Herculeah very glad she wasn't Samson-ya.

"Well, I was in Death's Door today—"

"The bookstore."

"Yes, and Uncle Neiman was telling me that you came to a signing for Mathias King."

"That I did."

"And you asked him some questions that seemed to make him uneasy."

"That they did."

"Well, I wanted to pick your brain about that. I want you to tell me everything you know about Mathias King."

"Even if it's unpleasant? I do not like that man."

"Especially if it's unpleasant," Herculeah answered firmly.

11

THE WORST WORD
IN THE ENGLISH LANGUAGE

It was very hard to get Rita Hayworth to return to the topic of Mathias King.

Herculeah and Gilda were now in Gilda's car. After they left the sun room, Gilda had said, "Oh, I've got to go into town and pick up something at the cleaners. I'll give you a lift and we can talk on the way."

"That would be great," Herculeah had said. "I came out on the bus, and I didn't take time to check the return schedule. I was in such a hurry to talk to you."

Gilda guided the car out of the parking lot at Magnolia Downs with one hand. "I have to tell you why I've got to go into town."

"Sure." Herculeah sighed. That wasn't what she wanted to talk about, but she was saving bus fare and a boring ride into town.

"Tomorrow night is stunt night at Magnolia Downs. And last stunt night I did my take-off on Rita Hayworth. In one of her movies she did a number called 'Put the Blame on Mame,' and she wore this slinky black dress and slinky long gloves, and it was sort of a striptease. So I got the video and I had Rita Hayworth on the TV screen doing her number and I did a sort of take-off in front of her. I know it's hard to imagine me in a slinky black dress, sexily removing my gloves and swinging them around in the air, but that was what was so funny. It was a hoot, which is about all you can hope to be when you're my age—I'm eighty-four."

She turned a corner, narrowly missing a bus. Herculeah remembered her wild ride with Uncle Neiman. She checked her seat belt.

"Anyway, everybody wants me to do it again, and my black dress and gloves are at the cleaners."

She sounded her horn at a pedestrian. "Now what was it you wanted to talk about?"

At last. "Mathias King," Herculeah said.

"Ah, yes. You want to know everything I know about Mr. King."

"Yes, I do."

"Actually most of what I have is suspicion."

"Me, too," Herculeah admitted.

"Well, Mathias King wrote a book called *A Slash of Life*."

"I reread most of it on my bus ride out here."

"Well, maybe it was just coincidence, but a very dear friend of mine since childhood, Rebecca Carwell, died in a similar way."

"Stabbed?"

"Yes, but that wasn't all. The house he described was like her house. No, it *was* her house. And there were details about the house that he couldn't have known about unless he had been inside it. The burgundy damask curtains, the huge Buddha in the entrance hall. The more I read the book—and I've read it four or five times—the more certain I become that he knew Rebecca."

"Maybe he did."

"But it's still only a suspicion." She ran one hand through her bowl haircut. "He came out to Magnolia Downs a few years ago—he did a magic show one evening after supper. This was before he became the Murder King."

"He did a little magic in Hidden Treasures yesterday. He almost choked my friend."

"He's quite good, but what I've been trying to remember is whether Rebecca was there that evening. She frequently came out to have supper with me, and if she was there for the magic show, it would be just like her to look him up later."

"I can tell that you miss your friend."

"I do." She broke off abruptly and said, "You know I just had an inspiration."

"Oh?"

"I have a key to Rebecca's house. The house was closed for investigation, but it's on the market now, and it's exactly as it was when she died."

They were stopped at an intersection now, and Gilda turned her bright eyes to Herculeah.

"I haven't been inside the house since Rebecca was killed—I couldn't bring myself to go inside. But if you'd go with me ..."

"I'd like to see it."

"It might give us inspiration."

Herculeah glanced out the car window and straightened. She peered out the window as Gilda turned the corner.

"Oh, there's my friend—the one I was telling you about! He must be out of the dentist!"

"You want to pick him up?"

"No, just let me out! I've got so much to tell him."

"Are you sure it was your friend? You didn't get a very good look at him."

"I'd know my friend if I only saw him for a second. I'd recognize him from a mile away."

"He must be a very good friend."

"Oh, he is."

Actually, she had only seen the back of his head, but he was holding it in an upbeat, happy way, so his visit to the dentist probably hadn't been too bad. He would be glad to see her.

Gilda pulled the car over to the curb.

Herculeah said, "Thank you for the ride. And I would very much like to see the inside of the house where the murder occurred. Our phone's listed in my mom's name—Mim Jones."

"I'll give you a call."

"And can I bring my friend? He had to miss out on all this—going to Death's Door, doing Tai Chi—all because he had a stupid dentist appointment."

"Bring him along by all means."

"Thanks."

Herculeah swirled out of the car, shut the car door, and started running. She could call out Meat's name—that would stop him—but she always enjoyed taking him by surprise.

She got closer. Now she could see his shoulders—he was definitely in a good mood, because Meat's shoulders had a tendency to sag when things weren't going well. Then the crowd parted. She could see him clearly now and she could see that—

Her mouth dropped open in surprise. She stopped in place. She blinked as if to clear her vision. She could not believe what she saw.

As she stood there, frozen in place, she realized that Uncle Neiman had been right. Meat hadn't gone to the dentist at all. She remembered his exact words: "I thought Sears said he was going on a—"

And now at last, she could finish the sentence with what had suddenly become the most despicable word in the English language. Her brain seemed almost to spit out the word.

"—date."

Meat McMannis had gone on a date.

Then as he and the date were getting into the car, the date turned as if to say something to Meat. Instead she looked over her shoulder. Her eyes seemed to ignore the rest of the sidewalk crowd and focus directly on Herculeah.

Herculeah felt as if she was being appraised, appraised and found wanting, as if she were an item on the sale table at Hidden Treasures, as if there was a sign around her neck that read AS IS.

Then Meat and the girl got into the car, and the car pulled away from the curb. Herculeah stood there staring after the departing car.

Herculeah prided herself on her ability to maintain control no matter what the situation. But her body sometimes betrayed her. Her hair frizzled. Her throat tightened. Her blood ran cold. Her heart pounded.

Now her face was flushed. Herculeah didn't even have to put her hand up to her cheek to know it would be hot.

She kept standing there long after the car had disappeared in traffic. She would have kept standing there for the rest of her life, perhaps, if a car's horn hadn't sounded beside her.

A voice called, "Herculeah!" It was Gilda. "Want a ride home?"

Herculeah nodded.

She managed to get into the car.

"You looked as if something was wrong."

"Something was wrong," Herculeah admitted.

"It wasn't your friend."

"Well," she tried to smile, "let's just say it wasn't who I thought it was."

Gilda looked at her sharply. "I've got an idea," she said.

"Oh."

"Rebecca's house."

"Oh?"

"We could go there now." Herculeah had a blank look on her face, as if her mind was far away.

"The house where Rebecca was killed. We could go there now. Are you up for it?"

"I've got nothing better to do."

"Then we're off."

She pulled the car back into the stream of traffic, and with horns blaring their alarm, they headed for the murder house.

12

THE UNUSED HALF-SMILE

Although Meat would never, ever admit this to his mother, the date hadn't been that bad. At least, he could think of it as a date now instead of a life-threatening disease.

When his mother had told him about the arrangements, he had been beset by one fear after another. They had been like furious, uncontrollable ocean waves washing over him—each one more treacherous than the one before.

The first wave of fear, of course, had been that she would be an ogre. That she would be ugly was a given. Only very ugly girls would allow their aunt to arrange dates for them.

But, to his surprise, the girl had been pretty. Even with his limited knowledge of girls, he realized this was exactly what most girls wanted to look like—small and blonde, with white teeth and a turned-up nose, and encased in the lingering scent of some flower Meat had never smelled before.

Of course she wasn't what Herculeah wanted to look like,

because Herculeah wanted to look like herself. However, his thoughts continued, if Herculeah had had to look like someone else, this would have been his personal recommendation.

His next wave of fear had been that he would never have anything to say, that the afternoon would be one long painful silence after another broken only by her asking, "What are you thinking?" followed by the truly desperate "What are you thinking now?" But from the moment she got into the car, she had handled the conversation.

"Oh, thank you, thank you," she'd said. "I was soooo bored. I was afraid you'd refuse to take me to the movies and I'd have to go by myself, and while I was desperate, I wasn't that desperate."

Meat's mother was watching them in the rearview mirror, and she gave him a look. It was the look dog trainers gave their dogs before the command, "Speak!"

"It's not so bad."

"You've been to the movies by yourself?"

"Yes."

"But you're a guy. You can get away with stuff like that. You can go anywhere by yourself and nobody gives you looks like this."

She gave him a look of such pity and scorn that he had to admit to himself that there was probably no movie great enough to risk getting a look like that.

But now the date was almost over. They had had pizza, they had seen a movie, and now they were on their way home, sitting side by side in the backseat while Steffie leaned forward to describe, scene by scene, the movie they had just seen for Meat's mom.

"And I knew who was going to be mutated, didn't I, Albert?"

She poked Meat, and he said, "She did."

"And I knew who was doing the mutating, didn't I?"

"She did."

Actually nothing in the entire movie had taken him by surprise, because Steffie had predicted every single thing. Even after the woman behind them asked her to shut up, she continued her predictions in a whisper.

"I've always been like that. I always know what's going to happen. There's a word for what I am, but I can't think of it."

"Clairvoyant," Meat said.

"That's it! Your son is soooo smart. But I can only do it in the movies and on TV. In real life, I just bumble along not suspecting one single thing. Oh, are we here already?"

They pulled up in front of Steffie's aunt's house. Meat's mom gave him a look in the rearview mirror, and Meat got out dutifully, held the door for Steffie, and then walked her to the front door.

There Steffie said, "Oh, thank you, thank you. I was sooo bored. You want to do something tomorrow? We could go back and see that movie about the end of the world."

"I think Mom's got something planned."

"I'll call you tonight, okay?"

"Fine."

He went back, got in the car, and sighed with relief. He would spend the rest of the drive, he decided, practicing a half-smile that would, when he saw Herculeah, make her think he'd gotten Novocain on that side of his face at the dentist's office.

He didn't get to practice his half-smile for more than three seconds, because his mom glanced at him over her shoulder and said, "So what was Herculeah doing following you?"

"What? What do you mean 'following me'?"

"Well, I can't imagine what else the girl was doing. She was standing not ten feet away from you—I saw her in the rearview mirror. She watched you and Steffie get into the car, and she watched us drive away. I half expected her to run after the car like that dog we used to have."

Meat cleared his throat. "Let me get this straight. Herculeah saw me with Steffie."

"Yes."

"She saw us getting in the car?"

"Yes."

"I don't believe you," he said.

But even as he spoke, he recalled Steffie's words as they got into the car.

"Did you see that girl standing on the sidewalk watching us?"

He had said, "No."

"Well, I wish my hair was springy like that. All my hair will do is turn under."

And his mother had said, "I saw that girl. Your hair is a hundred times prettier than hers."

And Steffie had fluffed her hair and said, "Thanks," as if that was exactly the comment she had been fishing for.

He felt himself sinking into the car's upholstery, the way the Wicked Witch of the West shriveled up in *The Wizard of Oz*.

His mother was still talking, but his increasing misery had blocked out her words.

"And one thing more," his mother continued in a loud commanding voice. "Look at me, Albert."

Their eyes met in the rearview mirror. Due to the importance of this one thing more, she had not started through the intersection even though the light was green.

Horns blew behind them.

"I think you should make it clear to Herculeah that you have a life of your own to lead."

"I think that's a done deal," he said.

Satisfied, his mother steered the car through the intersection.

13

THE MURDER HOUSE

They pulled into the driveway of a large, two-story brick house with columns across the front. In the yard was a FOR SALE sign with the prominent name of the realtor on top.

Herculeah looked at the house. It had obviously been the home of people who were rich, but it was no mansion. Also, it did not have the look of a house where a murder would take place. However, it did resemble the house described in *A Slash of Life*.

Herculeah and Gilda got out of the car and crossed the well-kept lawn. Halfway to the steps, Gilda stumbled and stopped.

"Are you all right?" Herculeah asked.

"Yes, it's nothing. I just remember something that happened right here."

"It must have been something unpleasant, because your face is pale."

"I'm fine," she said firmly, and continued up the walk and up the steps. Herculeah followed.

"I'm glad they're keeping the place up," Gilda said as she fished in her large purse for keys. "This house is very important to me."

She put the key in the lock, turned it, and opened the door.

She hesitated as if entering the house was going to be very difficult. She took a deep breath.

"I'll go first, if you like."

"Please."

Herculeah stepped into the entrance hall. She was still in a sort of daze from seeing Meat and his date. Usually she felt that a house of murder had a special aura. The temperature was colder somehow—a ghostly chill perhaps. Today, in her numbed state, the air seemed ordinary.

She did notice that the inside of the house was the same as the house in *A Slash of Life*.

She glanced to the right. The large Buddha sat in a crevice in the wall. Herculeah recognized that it was made of jade and probably very valuable.

"Oh, here's the Buddha," Herculeah said. "You mentioned it earlier in the car, and this morning, Uncle Neiman told me that you specifically mentioned the Buddha at the book signing." Had it only been this morning? "It was in the book, and here it is in the house."

"Yes." Gilda stepped into the entrance hall and crossed to the Buddha. "Rebecca and I never left this house without rubbing our hands over Buddha's belly for luck."

She rested her hand on Buddha's belly. She sighed and turned away. She paused in an arched doorway. "Here's the parlor. We weren't supposed to play in here, but it was the perfect place for hide-and-seek."

"Is that where she was killed?"

"No, that happened in the library."

"We don't have to go in the library if that would upset you."

Ever since they had entered the house, she had felt Gilda becoming more and more anxious.

"I want to see it." She glanced at Herculeah with gratitude. "I could never do it without someone like you along for support. This is the last time I'm ever coming here, and it's a way of closing the book, of saying good-bye." She strengthened herself with a deep breath. "The library is this way."

They walked down the hall to a room, and Gilda opened the door.

The library was large and lined with books. But they weren't the kind of books that you read, Herculeah thought. They were rich-people books—leather-bound, with titles embossed in gold.

In the center of the room, facing the door, was a large, handsome desk. The divided front was carved with scenes of two famous people at their desks—Abraham Lincoln on the right, Shakespeare on the left.

Gilda interrupted Herculeah's thoughts. "She died at that desk," she said.

"Don't go in any farther," Herculeah advised. "You can say good-bye from here."

But, as if she was sleepwalking, Gilda moved into the room. Her steps on the thick Oriental carpet were soundless. Herculeah followed.

"This was her father's desk," Gilda said, "but after his death, it became hers. She was a lot like her father. That's his portrait behind the desk."

Herculeah glanced up at the oil painting of a man trying to look genial but failing because of the straight line of his mouth. "Did she resemble her father?"

"Somewhat. Her father was good to my mother and me. My mom was the housekeeper here for many years. Mr. Carwell left my mother money in his will—a lot of money. That's how I bought my apartment at Magnolia Downs."

The top of the desk was empty of items, the dark wood polished to a sheen. "There used to be a leather-edged blotter here," Gilda said, "a silver inkwell there, a silver box of cigars on the right. And, of course, the letter opener."

She fell silent.

"The police never found the murder weapon. Whoever killed her must have taken it with them. The only thing missing from the desktop was the letter opener. It was a long, thin stiletto that had come from Italy. It was very beautiful, and probably the murder weapon."

"Have you seen enough?"

Gilda didn't answer. She went and stood behind the desk, beside the leather chair with the same carving as the desk. "She was sitting here, and her murderer was standing about where I'm standing. The murderer probably picked up—"

For a moment Herculeah was back at Hidden Treasures watching Mathias King wielding his invisible "lovely stiletto." She remembered the way his long, thin fingers drew the blade in the air and then with a quick jab thrust it into a victim. Her hair frizzled. Her hair always frizzled to warn her something was about to happen.

"Gilda," Herculeah said firmly, "maybe we should go home."

Gilda glanced over at Herculeah. "You're right." Without glancing at the desk again, she crossed the room and into the hallway.

She paused at the Buddha. "I never left the house without rubbing Buddha's belly."

"Never?"

Gilda thought for a moment, and a cloud seemed to fall over her face. "Not that I remember."

She glanced back at the door to the library. "A person would have to be insane to kill a lovely woman like Rebecca."

Then with a final motion she rubbed her hand over Buddha's belly. As Herculeah moved for the door, Gilda said, "You don't need any luck?"

Herculeah smiled. She returned, rubbed Buddha's belly, and then led the way out of the house.

THE CURIOSITY GENE

"Bye, and thanks," Herculeah called as she got out of the car and shut the car door.

"It's I who am grateful to you," Gilda said. "I'll give you a call. We need to talk some more. You've helped me a lot." She waved good-bye as she drove away.

Herculeah turned and went up the steps without glancing over at Meat's house as she usually did.

As she unlocked the front door and entered the hall, her mom called from her office, "Who gave you a ride home?"

Herculeah went to the open double door to her mom's office. The room had once been the living room, but now it was Mim Jones's office. It was where she saw her clients.

There were two comfortable chairs facing her mom's desk, and Herculeah sat in the one facing the window. Now she could glance at Meat's house without being seen.

The house was dark. Meat must not have returned from his—her brain practically spit out the word—date.

"The nicest woman in the world gave me a ride home," she said.

"The nicest woman in the world?" her mom said, raising her eyebrows. "Nicer than your own mother?"

"Well, close," Herculeah said. "Her name's Rita Hayworth."

"Go on."

"But everybody calls her Gilda."

"So what did you do all day, hon? Are you all right? Your face looks flushed."

"I've had a busy day. I went to Death's Door to get some books and then I went out to Magnolia Downs and had a Tai Chi lesson and then—and then I went with Gilda to see the house her friend was murdered in."

"That's quite a day."

"I actually learned something at Tai Chi. Would you like to see me hold up the sky?"

"I've been seeing you do that your whole life."

Herculeah glanced out the window. She could see Meat's house, but nobody was looking out the window at her house. She hesitated.

She could have told her mom about Meat's treachery, and her mom would have been sympathetic. But it had been such an emotional moment that she didn't know how to describe it. She knew what it was not. It was not jealousy. It was not envy.

It was not any of those terrible emotions you read about in books.

However, until she figured out what the emotion was, she would keep it to herself.

"I think I'll take a shower," she said.

She got up and started for the door. Again she hesitated. She said, "But if I get a phone call—and I'm halfway expecting one—"

The phone rang, cutting off her comment.

"There's something wrong with this phone. It rings upstairs, but when I pick it up, I just get a dial tone." Her mom picked up the phone and held it out so Herculeah could hear the tone for herself.

"It's Tarot," Herculeah said.

"Tarot's learned to ring like a phone?"

"I'm afraid so. Next he'll be answering it. 'Mim Jones's office.'"

Her mom laughed at the imitation of Tarot. "Oh, wait a minute." She shifted some papers on her desk and then held up an envelope. "You've got mail." She sang out the words.

"I never get mail."

"And it looks like an invitation."

"I never get those either."

Herculeah crossed to her mother's desk and held out her hand. The envelope was a square of heavy cream-colored paper, and it was addressed in fine black script that looked almost like calligraphy. She had never seen the words "Miss Herculeah Jones" written more beautifully.

Her mom said, "It wasn't mailed—no stamp. Evidently someone put it through the mail slot. I found it when I got home. It was on top of the regular mail."

Herculeah turned the envelope over in her hand. The return address was One Kings Row. There was only one person she knew who would have an address like that.

She slipped her thumb under the flap of the envelope and worked it loose. As she reached in to withdraw the heavy cream-colored note card, she felt a faint frizzling in her hair.

She took out the card. On the front, in black ink, was the drawing of a house. It was a two-story house with a tall attic. The windows were shuttered, and there was a gate guarding the walkway up to the house. The tips of the iron fence posts were as sharp as sabers. Chimneys grew out of the roof, and guarding them were what appeared to be birds perched on the edge of the roof.

Herculeah opened the card.

Her mother watched as she opened it. The picture on the front of the card was exposed, and her mother studied the house.

"The house looks spooky," her mother commented. "Who does it belong to—the Addams family?"

"No, but it belongs to a man who's just about as spooky."

"So what's inside the note?" her mother asked.

"Oh, nothing."

"It must be something because it's taking you an awful long time to read it. Is it an invitation?" She laughed. "I'm curious."

"You're always curious."

"Well, so are you. I've caught you time and again in here going through my personal files."

"We're all curious," Herculeah said. "That's why you're a private investigator and why Dad's a police lieutenant. And I got a double dose of that curiosity gene. Anyway, you never will tell me anything. Why should I tell you all my stuff?"

"Because you know how horrible it is to be curious and not get an answer."

"That's true."

"So?"

"It is an invitation," she admitted.

"To what?"

Herculeah took a deep breath. "To a party," she said. She turned to the stairs and put her hand on the banister.

"I'm going to take a shower," she said. "Maybe I can wash away some of—" She paused.

She was going to say, "some of these bad emotions," but that would only pique her mom's curiosity.

"Some of what?" her mother asked, her curiosity already piqued.

"I really don't know."

Then, before her mother could get out another question, Herculeah rushed up the stairs.

15

LIES AND MORE LIES

"Hi, Herculeah, it's me. You won't believe what happened. Remember I was going to the dentist's office? Well, when I got there, the office was closed, and there was this girl there—she'd had an appointment, too, so my mom—you know how she is—took pity on her and insisted she . . .

"Hi, Herculeah, it's me. Guess what happened? My first cousin from Atlanta—I've probably mentioned her—came to town and on the way here she got a toothache, and Mom—you know how she is—insisted that she take my dental appointment and on the way home she—my mom—said . . ."

Meat was stretched out on the sofa working on some lies. From the TV in the corner of the room came the muted noises of all-star professional wrestling. Meat's dad, Macho Man, was in a life-and-death struggle with the Cyclone.

Usually when Meat watched this tape—even though he knew the outcome—he became anxious for his dad.

Today, however, he was in a life-and-death struggle of his own.

"Hi, Herculeah, it's me."

The phone rang.

"I'm not here!" he yelled to his mom in the kitchen.

He knew it was Steffie wanting to do something tomorrow. And although he'd been practicing lying all evening, he still hadn't mastered the art, and even if he did think of an excuse, his mom would be there to yell, "That's not true," into the phone. His mother had proven she could not be trusted.

Also, Steffie was used to getting her way. Herculeah might overlook his having one date, but it would be hard for anybody to overlook two. That was practically going steady.

"I won't lie for you," his mother warned from the kitchen. She came into the room and turned off professional wrestling as she always did. Apparently his mom preferred live entertainment.

Meat got up from the sofa quickly and stepped out on the front porch. "Now you don't have to lie," he called before he shut the door. "I'm really not here."

He waited on the porch for what seemed like an unusually long time, but then again, Steffie was a talker.

As he stood there, he went over his lies, and then a sudden thought stopped him. He did not need to lie. After all, Herculeah didn't know that he knew that she knew about the date. Or something like that.

And! Uncle Neiman was his uncle. His own uncle! She had

gone to his uncle's shop. Therefore it was his right, as a nephew, to find out what had happened.

He would take the straightforward approach. None of these confusing tales of girls in distress.

"How did it go at Death's Door?" he would say. "Did you get the Mathias King books from my uncle?"

He was fine-tuning this approach when his mother opened the door. "It's safe. You can come in now."

Meat entered the living room, turned on the TV, rewound the tape, and threw himself down on the sofa in his original pose.

"Thank you, Mom."

"You have to understand right now that I am not going to lie for you on the telephone."

She put her hands on her hips—a pose Meat did not care for. But, hey, he told himself, you owe her. She prevented you from having a phone conversation with Steffie. The only person he liked to talk to on the phone was Herculeah.

"I know, Mom. I don't expect you to. If it happens again, I'll go back out on the porch."

"Some girls just won't give up," his mom said.

He certainly agreed with that statement. "Steffie's the epitome of that type."

To himself he began practicing. "Hi, I was curious about how it went at my uncle's shop."

It wouldn't hurt to stress the words "my uncle." He was repeating the phrase when his mother paused in the doorway.

"Oh, that wasn't Steffie on the phone."

"It wasn't?"

"Steffie's mom is here. I called Dottie to find out what Steffie had said about the date, and Dottie said the wedding was off. That was why Steffie was here in the first place—because her mom was getting married for the third time."

Meat stopped practicing his straightforward approach. He sat up. His whole body was rigid with sudden alarm.

"It was your little friend across the street."

"Herculeah?"

"Yes. It was Herculeah."

16

THE CANDLES OF TRANQUILITY

Mathias King stood in the doorway to his Den of Iniquity. He inhaled the scent of the room with a sense of pleasure.

Rooms dedicated to murder, he felt, had their own special scent—the way a library did, or a doctor's office, or a hair salon, or ... well he could go on and on.

He stepped inside the room. He pressed the switch that flooded the room with light. The lights were concealed above the cabinets, for Mathias King liked to admire his possessions—but he would not use those lights when Herculeah came to tea. On that special occasion, a different lighting would be called for.

He did not let his eyes linger over his weapons as he usually did. The guns that had fired fatal bullets, the knives that had ended lives were ignored. Mathias King had something else on his mind—the Candles of Tranquility.

There were thirteen of the candles, placed around the room.

Some were in sconces on the wall, some grouped on tables, some in tall, wrought-iron candlesticks.

They were all blood red—"scarlet" the lady at the shop had called them, but Mathias King felt blood red was a more appropriate name in this room. The candles were the same color as the heavy draperies at the end of the room.

"These particular candles give off the scent of poppies," the lady had told him. "Some people have said the scent makes them tranquil."

"I am not a man who values tranquility," he had told the woman, "but perhaps some of my visitors would enjoy the sensation."

"I'll light one for you."

She had produced a match and lit the candle.

Mathias King breathed in the scent of poppies, smiled, and said, "As I suspected, I am a man who is immune to tranquility."

Mathias King cast his eyes over the entire room for one final time. Everything was in place. Everything was festive and inviting. He smiled, showing his pointed teeth.

The Den of Iniquity was ready for a tea party.

17

CONFERENCE CALL

Meat got up, instantly, manfully, from the sofa. He passed his mother without a glance and went directly to the telephone in the kitchen.

He punched in Herculeah's number with a stiff, accusing finger. He was pleased that his hand was as steady as his intention.

"Mim Jones," a voice answered.

"Hello, Mrs. Jones, it's me, Meat. I wanted to speak to Herculeah. I'm returning her call."

"Just a minute."

There was a pause. He could hear Mrs. Jones's footsteps. She was probably walking with the cordless phone to the foot of the stairs.

"Herculeah," she called. "Meat's on the phone. He wants to talk to you. Can you pick up?"

He could not hear Herculeah's answer, but Mrs. Jones said,

"I'm sorry, Meat. She can't come to the phone. She's in the shower."

"Well, did she happen to say what she was calling about, Mrs. Jones?" He was pleased that his tone of voice continued to be purposeful and businesslike, the voice of a person who had nothing to hide such as a date with Steffie.

Before Mrs. Jones could reply, he heard Herculeah's voice.

It did not sound as if the voice was coming from the shower. It sounded as if it was coming from the top of the stairs. Obviously Herculeah's mother did not have the same reservations about lying on the telephone as his mom.

"Ask him something for me," he heard Herculeah yell down the stairway.

"What?"

He steeled himself. Now Mrs. Jones would say Herculeah wanted to know what he was doing with a girl when he was supposed to be at the dentist.

And he knew that if he reverted to one of his lies, he would have to listen to Mrs. Jones repeat his lie up the stairs, and then he would have to hear Herculeah catch him in the lie. But then if he didn't lie, the truth being thrown back and forth on the stairs like a ball wouldn't be much better....

Meat began to feel dizzy, as if he were watching a fast Ping-Pong game.

As usual, Herculeah surprised him.

"Ask him if he got an invitation to the party." Again she was careful not to say it was at the Den of Iniquity. Her mom wouldn't let her go to a place like that.

"All right."

Mrs. Jones's voice came back on the phone. "Herculeah just wanted to know," she began, "if you received an invitation to—"

Before she could complete the sentence, Meat said, "No, I didn't get an invitation."

"I'll tell her." She called up the stairs, "No, Herculeah, he didn't get an invitation. Anything else?"

"No, Mom, that's all I wanted to know."

"That's all she wanted, Meat. Good night."

Mrs. Jones hung up before he was through with the conversation. He didn't even get to return her good night. He stood there, listening to the dial tone.

What he really wanted to do was give Mrs. Jones a warning. Meat remembered how interested Mathias King was in Herculeah. He didn't want her anywhere near him.

"Whatever you do, don't let your daughter accept any invitation from Mathias King. The man's a murderer."

THE PRINTOUT

"Mom, are you asleep?"

"Not anymore, Herculeah."

"Well, can I use your computer?"

"What's wrong with your own computer?"

"Nothing, only I don't have the program for looking up addresses. I just want to print out a quick map."

"I suppose there's no point in my asking what address it is you want to print out."

Herculeah sighed. "Just tell me yes or no."

"Well, if the address is One Kings Row, don't bother; I already printed it out myself."

"Mom! You read the back of my envelope."

"May I remind you again that I could have steamed the whole thing open and sealed it back if I'd wanted to. When I was half your age, I was an expert at steaming open envelopes illegally. My mom used to have me do it all the time when my dad received a suspicious letter. Dad never suspected a thing. I was that good."

"I would accuse you of steaming open my mail except that I don't get any."

"Also the name of the street rang a bell."

"You'd heard of the street before?"

"Yes."

"Did it have something to do with one of your cases?"

"I thought it might."

"Which one?"

"But then I thought maybe it rang a bell because there was a movie by that name."

"Mom, get to the point."

Her mom obviously had no intention of getting to the point. She said, "I lay here, thinking and thinking about it, and then I fell asleep, and when I woke up, I remembered."

"Tell me!"

"A couple of years ago I was contacted by the League of Women for Education. Every year, the league would have a tour of homes—they raised money for scholarships that way."

"Go on!"

"They'd get eight or ten homes and there was always a theme. One year it would be homes of artists, one year homes of the rich and famous, once it was musicians."

"Is that why they contacted you? They wanted to do a tour of homes of private detectives?"

Her mom laughed. Even though the room was dark—Herculeah had not turned on the light—she enjoyed her mother's smile.

"This was to be a Halloween tour. The theme was secret rooms, secret passages. The league contacted me because they weren't having any luck. I had a case at the library at that time—remember someone was ripping off books—and I got up a list of old houses that qualified and, if my memory serves me correctly, One Kings Row was on the list."

Herculeah was silent for a moment. Then she said, "Secret passage or secret room?"

"My memory doesn't serve me that well."

"But you did print the map?"

"I did."

"And did you find the house?"

"I did. Actually there's only one house on the street. It's marked on the map by a small red star, so you can't miss it."

"And will I go there by bus, by foot, by bicycle, or will you drive me?"

"Oh, bicycle."

"I was afraid of that."

"You can take the bike trail through the park."

"Good. I'll do that."

She turned to go back to her room, and her mom said, "Come sit down by me for a minute."

She patted the side of the bed, and Herculeah went over. The queen-size bed was the same bed her parents had shared when they were married. Her mom still slept on her own half. She shifted to make room for Herculeah, and Herculeah sat down.

"I'm a little worried about you."

"Oh, Mom, it's just a party."

"I'm not worried about that. I get the feeling that there's something more serious troubling you. And I don't like you to be troubled."

"Well—"

"Did you and Meat have a misunderstanding?"

"Well."

"Is that 'well' a 'yes'?"

"I guess so, but, Mom, this is something I have to figure out for myself."

"Are you sure you can figure it out?"

Herculeah smiled. "Hey, of course I can. I'm a detective, remember?"

19

ONE KINGS ROW

HAVE TEA WITH ME
IN THE DEN OF INIQUITY.
TOMORROW.
3:00.
REGRETS ONLY.
555–1313

The invitation wasn't signed, but it didn't need to be. The invitation was in Herculeah's pocket, folded in its envelope. She had seen it only once, but she didn't need to see it again. She knew the words by heart. She had memorized the picture of the house as well.

Herculeah had the ability to see something once—particularly if it was important—and remember it forever.

Now she stood at the entrance to Kings Row. The street sign was green, the street name in white letters, just like all the other city street signs. Yet she could see that this street was not like other city streets.

There were no sidewalks, no curbs. Trees, hundreds of years old, lined the sides, their branches meeting over the street and forming a gloomy arch.

She glanced at her Mickey Mouse watch. She loved this watch. Her dad had given it to her long ago as a reward for learning to tell time. She could recall how proud she had been to visit her dad at the police station and have everyone want to know what time it was. Sometimes her dad would have to help her a little.

She would say, "Mickey's little hand is on two, and his big hand is between the four and five."

"Are you saying it's two twenty-two, Herculeah?"

"Yes!"

And a very enthusiastic police applause would follow. Cops didn't have a lot to clap about, so they welcomed the chance.

Mickey indicated that the time was now five minutes before three. Time to get moving.

Herculeah pushed her bike forward. As she moved into the gloom, she moved her sunglasses up to the top of her head.

She paused again at the entrance gate to One Kings Row, and glanced up at the house. Herculeah didn't know enough about architecture to know Gothic from Grecian, but she could always recognize Ghoul. This house qualified as early nineteenth-century Ghoul.

If Meat were here, Herculeah thought with a sudden pang of loss, he would not approve of the house. He would immediately comment on the round window in the attic.

"The house has a Cyclops's face," he would say, "and that one eye is staring at us right now."

She sighed. Of course, Meat wasn't here, and she had begun to wonder if he would ever be with her again. Still, he would have been right about that round eye in the attic—the only unshuttered window in the house. It did seem to be watching her.

She continued to push her bike forward. The crunch of her tires on the gravel drive was the only sound in the afternoon stillness. Even the traffic on the street was silenced by the thick foliage of the trees.

Ahead, parked beside the house, was a long black car. It did not surprise Herculeah that Mathias King's choice of wheels seemed to be a hearse.

She stopped behind the hearse and kicked down her bike stand. She glanced up once again at the tall, forbidding house, and then down at her watch.

Mickey's little hand was on the three and his big hand was pointing straight up.

"Are you saying it's exactly three o'clock, Herculeah?"

With a smile—not of anticipation but of remembrance—she swept up the stairs and paused at the door.

The knocker on the huge front door was in the shape of a dagger. She was disappointed that she was no longer surprised at anything.

She lifted the dagger and knocked.

20

DEN OF INIQUITY

"Welcome, dear Herculeah."

Mathias King gave a sweeping gesture of one arm that drew her into the hallway. She looked around, taking in the long hallway, the rooms on either side.

He seemed to shrug off the rooms. "The first floor of my home is of no interest," he said. "Living room, dining room, den, study, library, bedroom, kitchen, and so on." He gestured to the rooms on either side of the hallway.

Herculeah thought all the rooms were of interest. Behind any one of those paneled walls could be the entrance to a secret room or passage. Behind any one of those huge oil paintings could be a place to spy through the canvas. Any one of these huge carved chests could contain secrets from the past.

"The upstairs is of primary interest. It contains all my projects. Come."

Another gesture led her to the stairs. Mathias King seemed to have a way of getting just what he wanted.

Mathias King was, once again, all in black. Over his black pants and turtleneck shirt was a loose jacket with many pockets. "Never trust a magician with lots of pockets," she told herself.

"Did you say something, my dear?"

"Just to myself."

"I must warn you that I have very good ears. My pockets are empty, my dear."

She glanced over her shoulder at him and gave him a skeptical look with her gray eyes, but she said nothing.

"With eyes like that," he commented, "words are unnecessary."

As they stepped off the stairs, Mathias King said, "This way," and led her to a room at the front of the house. The window overlooked the hearse parked below.

"Here is where I write my books," he said. "I write all in longhand, and then I take my manuscripts, in fear and trembling that they will be lost to posterity, to a secretary."

"No computer?"

"Yes, I have a computer, but only to visit the Internet. You must have a computer. All your generation does."

"Yes."

"You can visit my Web site at your leisure."

"Let me guess," she said, "murder_king.com."

"I'm getting too obvious."

"Well, it's easy to remember."

They moved down the hall to the next room. "This room," he said, throwing open the door, "is my Magic Room."

Herculeah stood in the doorway. She had no desire to go inside the room. It was crammed with mirrored devices of all kinds, decorated boxes, hats, capes, and cages.

"Pay particular attention," he said, "to the golden sacrificial altar in the center of the room."

Herculeah looked at the altar. Pagan pictures and letters adorned the sides. Leather straps dangled over the sides of the pagan pictures.

"And why do I need to pay particular attention to the sacrificial altar?" she asked.

"Because, my dear, it will be the site of your murder."

She turned her steely gray eyes to his. "My murder?"

"Your literary murder," he corrected himself.

"Even literarily, I am not getting on any sacrificial altar."

He smiled, showing his pointed, animal teeth. "I was afraid you were going to say that. But as a special favor to me?"

"I don't owe you any favors."

She hesitated a moment, eyeing the altar. Strangely enough, her hair was not frizzling. She felt as if she were playing a game—a dangerous game, perhaps, but as long as she played by the rules, she felt she would be safe. Never let anyone know you're afraid of them, she reminded herself.

"Seen enough?" Mathias King asked.

"More than enough."

He closed the door and moved to the next. "Now for the Den of Iniquity."

"And tea," Herculeah reminded him.

"Ah, yes, I had forgotten. Tea."

He opened the door, and for a moment, all she could see was the blazing lights of candles. She smelled the scent of wax and something she could not identify—some sort of foreign incense, perhaps.

She stepped into the room, followed by Mathias King, and the candles seemed to have been placed so that they threw shadows on the wall. The corners of the room were in darkness.

"Don't you have an overhead light?" Herculeah asked. "I want to see this stuff."

"This stuff, as you put it, is best viewed in a soft, mysterious light. But, I assure you, my dear, you will perhaps see more than you like. Come."

21

TRAPPED

Herculeah and Mathias King proceeded slowly down the left side of the room.

"My old murders," he said with a gesture toward the display cases.

Glass-fronted cabinets lined the wall. The cabinets contained weapons, newspaper clippings, letters, and more—all pertaining to a particular murder. Most of the murders had taken place long ago, and Herculeah had never heard of the cases or the victims.

Beneath the glass cases were drawers and a white golden-edged card with lovely writing that Herculeah recognized as Mathias King's identifying the contents of each by case. The Ahitmore case. The Elison case. The murdered monk.

"You aren't interested in my real-life murders?" Mathias King asked.

"I guess I never heard of any of them."

"I'm sure your father has."

"Probably." She gave him a quick glance. "You'll have to invite him for tea."

"Perhaps."

At the end of the room was a wall completely covered by a heavy red drapery. "Let's open the curtains and let some light and air in here," Herculeah suggested.

"Light would spoil our mood."

"But some air would—"

"Come, this is what you came to see," Mathias King interrupted, speaking quickly as if to distract her from opening the draperies.

She eyed the draperies as they passed. She wondered if there was something behind them he didn't want her to see.

"These three tables contain all the things pertaining to my mystery novels. I haven't had cases built for them yet.

"This first table contains everything from *A Sip of Death*. The manuscript—see, it's all in my own handwriting as I said. And here is the cup I bought at Hidden Treasures."

"But there's no snake on it."

"Here's the one with the snake. I had a silversmith make it for me. The weapons I buy at Hidden Treasures—though I wouldn't hurt Mrs. Jay's feelings for the world—are seeds. I see them and my mind begins to nurture them and let them grow."

They moved to the next table. "*A Slash of Life*. I have the feeling that interests you most of all."

"Yes, it does. I spoke to a woman who felt you were somehow involved with the murdered woman."

"Did she now? Some people will claim anything to get attention."

"I didn't get the feeling she was that kind of woman."

"This is the letter opener I bought at Hidden Treasures, a mere seed of the knife over there that did the murder." He pointed to the center of the table.

There lay a knife nestled in the folds of a black silk scarf. Herculeah reached out her hand to push aside the silk so that she could get a better look at the knife.

"Don't touch that," he said quickly.

"Why not?" she asked, but he had spoken so forcefully she had already withdrawn her hand.

"I have reason to believe the fingerprints of the murderer are still on the knife."

"This is the knife that actually committed the murder? This is not a knife you had made up by some silversmith?"

His statement did not make sense to her. Perhaps it was the smell of the candles that was causing her confusion. She had never cared for artificial scents.

"I believe so. Even I, clever as I am, could not produce real blood on the blade of the knife."

"So this *isn't* the knife you bought at Hidden Treasures. Mrs. Jay doesn't have anything this fine."

"Perhaps it is a substitute for that knife."

Before she had time to form another question, he had guided her to the next table. "Now this table is the most important to the two of us. It concerns the murder in which you will participate."

Herculeah didn't want to leave the table for *A Slash of Life*. She still had questions, if only she could remember what they were—but she couldn't seem to help herself.

"The weapon"—he picked it up—"will be a sacrificial dagger."

She blinked her eyes so she could make out the dagger. It seemed to be wavering in the candlelight.

"In the book, you, my dear, will be the magician's assistant. I, of course, will be the magician."

He twirled the dagger in a masterful, threatening way.

"We will be doing an act. The act consists of a trick where I pretend to stab you, but this is a trick dagger. The blade recedes into the hilt on forceful contact." He acted out his part of the trick, striking the table hard enough for the blade to disappear.

"You didn't get that at Hidden Treasures."

"No, my dear, I got the sacrificial altar there. It was used in a play. But now, back to the trick. Unbeknownst to us, someone has rigged the dagger so that it will not collapse and it has become a lethal weapon. Someone, you see, wants you dead, my dear."

"I've got to get out of here," Herculeah said.

"I deliver a lethal blow with the knife. Naturally, I am accused of murder while the real murderer—"

"I've got to get out of here," she said again.

"No, no, my dear, you need tea. Sit! Sit!" He fairly pushed her into a chair and, although she didn't want to, she sat.

"I'll be right back with the tea. Lemon and sugar?" he asked.

"I don't care."

He was in the doorway and she was just ready to say, "Don't close the door," when he did.

She heard the door close and then a faint click as if it had been locked. She got up quickly, crossed the room, and tried the door. It did not open. She was locked in.

And the scent from the candles was really getting to her. She swirled and ran to the heavy drapes at the end of the room.

She thrust them aside, ready to open the windows, even with force if she had to. She'd break the glass with the heel of her boot.

The curtains parted, and Herculeah stood facing the paneled wall.

She noticed three things:

1) There was no door in the wall.

2) There was no window in the wall.

3) She was trapped.

22

AFTERNOON NIGHTMARE

Since Saturday, Meat had been in one of two places. He was either at the window watching for Herculeah, or he was lying on the sofa thinking about her.

At present, there was no point in being at the window. Herculeah had come out of the house at ten minutes past two, gotten her bicycle from the garage, and, without a glance in his direction, ridden off.

Knowing she had gotten an invitation, he had suspected she would be going out this afternoon. He had decided to follow her, but his plans were foiled when she got on her bike.

It was very hard to follow someone unnoticed on a bike, particularly when your bicycle was adorned with Day-Glo strips (his mother's work) so that he would be singled out from all other traffic.

Therefore, he was lying on the sofa, clicking the remote from channel to channel. He paused for a moment on the Disney

Channel. *Pinocchio* was on. Meat didn't feel up to watching a movie about a boy who'd paid dearly for his lies. It came too close to his own situation.

Coming up on the TV screen was the scene on Pleasure Island where the boys began to turn into donkeys. Meat had never liked this part. Even as a child, as he sat in the theater laughing with all the other kids, he had not found it funny.

He punched the MUTE button and closed his eyes, but kept his face turned toward the TV. It wouldn't hurt to check Pinocchio's progress every now and then.

He was almost asleep when he felt something lumpy resting under his head against the pillow. He tried to adjust the pillow. The lump got bigger. He lifted his head.

A long ear! He had grown an ear just like the boys on TV. And another ear on the other side.

He shared the horror of the mutating boys on the screen. No MUTE button could deaden the sounds of those terrible donkey screams, and he screamed right along with them.

And now he was sitting on something bumpy. Not a tail! Please, please don't let it be a tail.

He eased a hand beneath him, and of course it was a tail. It was such a forceful tail that it had split his pants open and was sprouting like a stalk of corn.

He got up at once. He had one goal, one chance to become a boy again. He had lied, and lying was just as bad an offense as those committed by the boys on the screen—smoking cigars and playing pool. He had to cross the street and retract that lie.

His hand had become a hoof, so it was difficult to open the front door, but he was so desperate he managed.

He tripped going down the steps—again, hoofs weren't made for steps—and crossed the street.

He was on all fours now, but at least that allowed him to gallop. He galloped across the street without being run over, and up the stairs to Herculeah's house. He punched the bell with his long nose and almost at once—to his great relief—Herculeah opened the door.

All he had to do now was say two words, "I'm sorry."

He threw back his head and brayed two words into her startled face.

"Hee-haw!"

Meat woke up in a cold sweat. He clasped his hands to his face, actually expecting to feel the features of a donkey. They were the features of a donkey, all right—but a human one.

He opened his eyes.

On the screen, Pinocchio was dancing with Gepetto and Figaro, and Cleo was splashing happily along to the music in her fish bowl.

"After you become a real boy, pal," Meat warned Pinocchio, "your troubles are just beginning."

23

THE CURTAINS' SECRET

Herculeah stood looking up at the heavy curtains. She was breathing through her mouth now.

Something bothered her about the curtains, but she had to struggle to think what it was. Her mind was becoming fogged.

She squinted up at the heavy folds.

The opening. It had something to do with the opening.

She recalled that when she had thrust the curtains aside, she had had a moment's difficulty in finding the opening. It was off-center.

That was strange. Why would the opening be off-center unless ... unless there was a reason. And the reason, she thought, had to be that there was something directly behind the opening.

She thrust the curtains aside again, but again saw only a bare paneled wall.

Frustrated by the sight, she was suddenly filled with the strength that often came from anger and frustration. She was furious at the man who had invited her here, who had tried to get her on a sacrificial altar and then locked her in a room full of suspicious candles—so furious that she could accomplish anything.

She would show Mathias King.

She felt the way Hercules must have felt during his labors. Hercules probably felt like this just before he diverted whole rivers, before he made mountains. Strengthened by the thought, she lifted her hands, grabbed fistfuls of drapery, and pulled.

With a tearing sound, the curtains came free of the rod that held them and fell. Herculeah was momentarily enveloped in the heavy cloth.

She threw it off. She grabbed a candle from a holder behind her and held it up to the wall with one hand. With the other, she tested the wall, knocking on it, trying to find where it sounded hollow.

There! And there! All along this strip of paneling.

Now she could see the faint crevice in the wood. She looked down, then up, then from side to side, trying to find some way of opening the door. There was nothing. Perhaps there was some knob hidden in the room, some piece of molding to turn—

She gave a frustrated yelp.

She didn't have time to look for it. If Mathias King's hearing was as keen as he claimed, he might have heard the draperies being ripped from the wall. She had no time to waste.

A girl's gotta do what a girl's gotta do.

Herculeah stepped back. The only other hidden staircase she had been involved with had been at Dead Oaks. And there hadn't been any special knob to turn there. She had been hiding in an old dressing room, and she had pressed back against the wall and fallen into the staircase. These things were not made of steel.

She pulled back her leg. And like someone from a kung fu exhibition, she gave a mighty kick.

Wham!

The wood splintered, and then, with a sigh, as if in surrender, the door revolved and opened.

Herculeah took in her first breath of decent air. It smelled faintly of dampness and mold, but it was better than what she had been breathing. She felt revived.

She lifted her candle into the opening. She saw a narrow flight of stairs leading down into the darkness.

Herculeah didn't hesitate. If Mathias King had not heard the draperies being ripped from the wall, he had certainly heard his precious door being kicked open.

Herculeah started down the stairs.

She had no idea where she was going, or what she would find at the bottom of the stairs, but anything was better than being at the mercy of the Murder King.

ESCAPE

The stairs were steep, but Herculeah had always been sure-footed. Still, she resisted the impulse to take them two or three at a time. This was not the time to fall.

At the bottom of the stairs there was a small landing. A barred door blocked her way.

Curtains, doors, bars. Nothing was going to stop her.

She lifted the first bar and tossed it on the stairs. She threw the second bar after it.

She could smell fresh air, and she knew that this door led to the outside. She pushed. The door resisted. She pushed again, and this time the door yielded a few inches.

She could see two inches of daylight. She inhaled the sweet air of afternoon.

She could see now that this door had not been used in a long time—years, perhaps. Leaves and dirt had built up against it. She put her shoulder to it, and the door creaked open a few more inches.

One more shove, and she was out.

She paused. Now she was clearheaded, and she had her first thought worthy of a girl named Herculeah. She thought, Why didn't I think to bring the knife? It has the murderer's fingerprints on it. Now Mathias King has time to get rid of it.

From the top of the stairs came a faraway but plaintive cry. "Come back. Oh, my dear, please come back."

"Yeah, right, come back and let you make a sacrifice out of me."

Going back for the knife was not an option. Getting out of here as fast as possible was.

She ran around the house. She knew she could get to her bicycle before Mathias King could get down the stairs and out the front door.

She grabbed her bike on the run, kicked up the stand, and took off down the drive.

"Wait! Wait!" Mathias King called after her, but she was already on the street.

At the head of the stairs, Mathias King turned and went back into the Den of Iniquity. He took in the damage.

The velvet curtains had been pulled down with such force that there were tears from the hooks. The door, which had stood undamaged for a hundred and fifty years, was ruined. The mark of Herculeah's boot was indented deeply in the wood.

"Oh, my dear," he said to the empty stairway. "The candles of tranquility didn't make you very tranquil, did they?"

And he went around the Den of Iniquity, blowing out the candles one by one.

BACK TO THE DEN OF INIQUITY

Herculeah took the bike trail through the park on the way home. She took it because it was quicker, but also because she feared that Mathias King might try to follow her in the hearse.

When she got home, she put her bike in the garage and started up the steps.

The phone began to ring. She knew it would be Meat calling to find out how the afternoon had gone. She knew he would be watching from the front window, so she took her time opening the door and going inside.

When she picked up the phone, she was surprised to hear Gilda's voice.

"Oh, I'm so glad I got you," Gilda said. "I just went by Rebecca's house and there was a SOLD sign in the yard. I called the realtor on my cell phone and guess what?"

"Gilda—"

"It's been bought by someone who's going to turn it into a

bed-and-breakfast! Isn't that wonderful? Now it will be a happy house again with—"

"Gilda!" This time her voice was so forceful that Gilda stopped.

"Is anything wrong?"

"Yes, I'm just back from Mathias King's house."

"You went there?"

Somehow Herculeah got the feeling Gilda wasn't that surprised.

"Yes. He's got a room called the Den of Iniquity, and in that room is the very knife that killed your friend."

There was a silence that continued so long Herculeah said, "Are you still there?"

"Yes."

"I was locked in the room with the knife and I had to break my way out. I was all the way outside before I realized that I should have brought the knife with me. Why did I leave it? Now Mathias King can get rid of it, and we have no proof he was the murderer."

"We have to go back and get it."

"No, he's in the house."

"I'll call him on my cell phone and see if he's there."

"I know the number," Herculeah said. "I remember it from the invitation."

She gave Gilda the number and waited while the phone rang on and on at One Kings Row.

"He's not there. This is our chance."

"I don't know about this."

"Can you get us inside the—what was it? Den of Iniquity."

"If that outside door's still open."

"Let's find out. I'm not far from your house. I'll pick you up."

"I just need to leave a note for my mom."

Herculeah wasn't sure this was a good idea, but she didn't have a better one. So when Gilda honked her horn, she ran out and got in the car.

They drove quickly to Mathias King's street with Herculeah pointing the way.

"You can't see the house from here," Herculeah said at the entrance to Kings Row. "Park here and let's slip through the trees."

They went through the trees together, keeping out of sight.

"The hearse is gone," Herculeah said. "It was parked right there."

"Then let's go."

"But what if he moved the hearse, put it in a garage or something, and is in the house waiting for us?" Herculeah said.

"We'll take that chance."

Herculeah had pretty much taken all the chances she wanted to for one day, but she led Gilda around the side of the house.

"The door's still open."

"We're going to get that knife," Gilda said.

As they walked toward the door, Herculeah said, "I don't understand why a house would have stairs leading outside."

"Oh, it's not strange at all. Victorian gentlemen were very secretive—didn't want their wives to know their comings and goings. They'd go into the room, ask not to be disturbed, and go out carousing. You lead the way up the stairs."

"The stairs are steep. Be careful."

Herculeah wasn't as afraid with Gilda on her side. That woman was very strong. She had seen that in Tai Chi class.

The door at the head of the stairs was as Herculeah had left it. She slipped through and stepped over the fallen curtain. Gilda followed.

"Now, where's the knife? Where's the knife?" Gilda said.

"On the middle table."

They walked to the table, and Gilda froze.

"That is the knife, isn't it?" Herculeah asked.

"It's the knife."

She looked closely at Gilda. Gilda was very pale. It was as if all the blood had drained from her head.

"Are you all right? You look like you're going to faint. Don't faint, because I could never get you and the knife back down those stairs."

Gilda didn't answer.

"We shouldn't have come. It's too much for you to see the actual knife—"

As if in a trance, Gilda stretched out her hand toward the knife.

"Don't pick it up," Herculeah said.

But Gilda paid no attention to Herculeah's warning. Her hand hovered over the knife.

Herculeah said, "No! No! You'll mess up the fingerprints. You'll ruin everything."

"Don't worry about that, Herculeah."

Herculeah glanced around the tabletops, looking for something. She said, "We need to get something firm—this manuscript cover ought to do it. I'll slide this under the knife and the scarf. We won't even fold the scarf over the knife. We don't want to do anything that would erase Mathias King's print."

"You don't have to worry about his prints."

"But that's the whole reason we're here—to get Mathias King's fingerprints on the knife."

"You won't find Mathias King's prints on the knife."

"Why?"

"Because the prints on the handle of the knife are not his."

"Then whose?"

Gilda turned and looked at Herculeah. Her face was still pale, but in the vague light that filtered through the open doorway, her eyes burned with the intensity Herculeah had last seen in the library of the murder house.

It was as if a mask had slipped from her face, and Herculeah's blood froze at what was revealed.

"The fingerprints on the knife," she said, "are mine."

THE HEARSE

"Could you tell me what a hearse is doing in front of the Jones's house?"

"A hearse?"

Meat went to the window. You could count on this happening. You stood at the window staring at nothing for an hour, then you went to the refrigerator for ten or fifteen minutes and a hearse drove up.

"It was here the other day, too," Meat's mother said as he joined her at the window. "A man got out—a very suspicious-looking man, I might add. He was all in black."

"Mathias King," Meat whispered.

"He went up the steps, dropped something in the mail slot, and left."

"Has he gotten out of the hearse today?"

"He went up the steps, rang the bell, got no answer, and got back in the hearse. He's still there."

Now Meat could see Mathias King's profile in the front seat of the hearse. He was staring straight ahead.

"I don't like it," Meat's mother said. "It gives the street a bad name. It's as if the man's waiting for someone to die."

"I'll find out what's going on," Meat said.

"I'll go with you."

"I'll do this myself."

He spoke so manfully that his mother nodded. Meat went out the door alone, crossed the street, and rapped on the window.

Mathias King rolled down the window and stared up at Meat with his black eyes.

"What are you doing here?" Meat asked bluntly.

"I'm waiting for Herculeah."

"Why?"

"Oh, dear. She was at my house for tea and I scared the girl. I didn't mean to. It was the last thing in the world I wanted to do."

Meat waited. He knew there was more.

"I get carried away. First I showed her the sacrificial altar. And I indicated—I didn't insist—I just indicated that I wanted her to get on it. I felt it would inspire me."

"And that scared her, so she left."

"There's more. Then we went in the Den of Iniquity, and I was explaining that she would be in my next mystery—she would be the next victim."

"And that scared her, and she left."

"There's more. Then I locked her in the Den of Iniquity."

"And that scared her and she left."

"Hurriedly," Mathias King said. He sighed. "I have to apologize to the girl. I really carried the whole thing too far."

"I agree."

"I thought she might be home by now. Maybe she is and she just won't come to the door. Could you go up and try? She might open the door for you."

"She's not home."

"Where is she?"

"I don't know. A woman picked her up in her car about a half hour ago. They haven't come back."

"A woman?"

"Yes."

Mathias King's eyes sharpened. "What did she look like?"

"Well, I couldn't see much—she didn't get out of the car—but she had white hair, and it was cut sort of like a monk's."

"Herculeah's in danger. Get in."

"In the hearse?"

"Get in! You want to save your friend's life, don't you?"

"That would make up for a lot," Meat admitted.

"Then get in!"

27

THE SACRIFICIAL DAGGER

"Your fingerprints?" Herculeah asked. She didn't want to believe it, but the crazed look on Gilda's face made it true.

"Yes, my fingerprints."

"Wait a minute. Are you saying your fingerprints are on the knife because . . . because"—she could hardly get out the words—"because you killed her?"

"Yes."

"You killed your friend."

"Yes."

"But why?"

"Do you remember when we were in Rebecca's house? When we were leaving, I said that only a person who was insane could kill someone like Rebecca."

"I remember."

"Well, that's what it was like—insanity. I didn't mean to. I didn't plan to kill her. I don't even remember doing it."

"How did it happen?"

Herculeah was relieved to see that Gilda had not actually picked up the knife, and had withdrawn her hand. Herculeah knew Gilda had murdered with that knife. Once it was in her hand, she wouldn't hesitate to use it again.

She had to keep her talking. Maybe Mathias King would come home. Maybe something would happen. She knew she could always dart around Gilda and beat her to the stairs, but she would have to leave the knife! With the fingerprints!

"She was like a sister to you," Herculeah said.

"Oh, yes. She was the older sister. She handed down her clothes to me. My mother was housekeeper there—did I mention that? I wore her cast-off clothes, and she never let me forget it. In front of our friends, she would say things like, 'I always wore that blouse with the top buttons open. It showed off my gold chains.'"

"She doesn't sound like much of a friend to me."

"She was a very greedy girl. She had everything, but like so many greedy people, she wanted it all."

"I don't understand people like that."

"If I got a friend, Rebecca would move heaven and earth to get the friend away from me. And she had the money to do it. I thought when we went to high school that I would be free of her. She was going to an expensive private school, but at the last minute, it was decided that I would attend the private school, too—it was a gift from her parents. My mother wouldn't let me refuse—she said it would be ungrateful."

Herculeah took a step backward, away from the table with the knife. Gilda followed, too intent on her story to notice she was being led away from her weapon.

"All my life it was like that. The first real happiness I had in life was at Magnolia Downs. I made real friends. I had a nickname for the first time in my life. I was Gilda. People liked me. I had my Tai Chi class."

"But if you were so happy—"

Gilda interrupted. "I wasn't going to be happy for long."

"Why? What happened?"

"On that day—the day of the murder—Rebecca asked to see me. She said she had a surprise.

"I went and she was in the library at her desk. Spread out before her were papers.

"'Look,' she said. I walked around the desk and looked down.

"'Isn't it wonderful!' she said. 'I'm going to be at Magnolia Downs with you. I've bought the Magnolia suite. They're renovating it for me. It has a lovely living room.' She pointed to the picture of a beautiful, spacious room. She said, 'I can have parties there, and—I was saving this for a surprise, but I have to tell you. It's too good to keep. I've been taking Tai Chi classes. I have a private teacher and I've caught on so quickly I'll be able to help you teach your classes.'

"And I remember nothing of the next few moments. I only know that I looked down and there was a knife in my hand and

Rebecca had been stabbed—I had just stabbed her once—and she was dead."

Herculeah took another measured step backward. She held her breath. Yes! Gilda followed.

"I ran out of the house. The knife was still in my hand, and I flung it aside. I got into my car and drove away. On the way home I lost control of the car and struck a tree. I wasn't wearing a seat belt—I was too upset—and my face struck the steering wheel. When I got back to the Downs I was in shock, trembling, incoherent—and bloody. I got a lot of sympathy for my accident, and the nurse checked me into the infirmary at once."

"Did the police come?"

"No, it wasn't a serious accident."

"I meant about the murder."

"Rebecca's body wasn't discovered until Monday, when the maid arrived. From Friday till Monday I was in and out of consciousness. I kept calling her name—Rebecca, Rebecca. And they tried to reach her—everyone at the Downs knew she was my best friend—but of course they couldn't. I had such dreams that I actually believed the murder hadn't happened."

"Until the police came."

"Yes, I knew what I'd done then, and I expected I would be arrested. My prints were on the knife, but that was the strange thing. They didn't find the knife. I had thrown it on the lawn in full view of anyone who came up the walkway, but they didn't find it."

"And they never found it."

"No. If they had, I would have been arrested."

"But your clothes! Her blood must have been on your clothes. Didn't the police ask about that?"

"By the time the police came to the Downs, the clothes had been washed, and all traces of blood—hers and mine—had disappeared."

"That's quite a story," Herculeah said. "You got away with murder."

"Not yet I haven't. That's why I'm here."

Herculeah's hair was beginning to frizzle. That meant the danger was real.

"I'm going to take the knife"—she glanced back to the table where it lay—"I'm going to wipe off my prints, and put it where it will be sure to be found."

"Like where?" Herculeah asked.

She didn't like the look on Gilda's face. It was as if another person had taken over her body, her mind. Her eyes glowed with madness.

Like in my chest? Herculeah thought. Surely not.

"Then I will depart—alone—and your body will be found in Mathias King's Den of Iniquity, and he will be the prime suspect."

Herculeah glanced aside. Now she was beside the last table. And there was the sacrificial dagger that Mathias King had hoped to embed in her chest.

"You're not going to stab me with that little letter opener," Herculeah said with a loud, scornful laugh. Startled, Gilda turned to look at her. "Sure it worked last time, but your friend was unarmed. And I'm not unarmed. I've got a dagger."

She picked up the sacrificial dagger and waved it in Gilda's face. Gilda's fevered eyes followed every movement.

When she goes for the dagger and tries to stab me, I'm throwing her to the floor, grabbing the murder knife, and I'm outta here, Herculeah thought.

"That is a better weapon," Gilda said.

She came closer to Herculeah, and Herculeah could imagine this was how she had looked before stabbing her friend.

Gilda reached out, wrested the dagger from Herculeah, and with a cry of triumph, thrust it at Herculeah's chest. Herculeah was just ready to throw her to the ground when she heard a scream at the door. It sounded like Meat.

She looked. Mathias King and Meat arrived just in time to see the thrust.

Herculeah's face was turned to them, and Meat knew it was the last time he would ever look into those hauntingly beautiful gray eyes.

She uttered what he knew would be her last word. "Meat."

28

WRAP-UP

"I still can't believe she's alive," Meat told the room for the fourth time. "I mean, you see somebody get stabbed like that, they stay stabbed." He turned back to Herculeah. "I still can't believe you're alive!"

"It was a fake dagger, Meat." She had explained this a lot, too. "The blade went up in the hilt. That's why I suckered her into using it instead of the knife. I wanted to preserve the finger-prints. Also, I felt that if she'd killed with that knife once, she wouldn't hesitate to do it again."

"I still can't believe you're alive."

"Could we get on with this?" Chico Jones said. Herculeah had called her father, and he was here in his official capacity.

They were gathered in the living room at One Kings Row. Herculeah and Meat sat side by side on a sofa. Mathias King stood leaning against the back of the chair in front of the fire-place. He had a faint smile upon his face as if he was enjoying the whole thing immensely.

Chico Jones sat at a table, and on the other side of the table sat his sergeant, taking notes.

Rita Hayworth had been driven to the police station, where she would be charged with assault and, if the fingerprints on the knife turned out to be hers, with the murder of Rebecca Carwell.

"I think I've got most of it except for a few points."

He looked up at Mathias King with his official expression. Chico Jones's stock in trade was never letting anyone know what he was thinking, but Herculeah could tell that Mathias King was not off the hook.

"Mr. King, how did you come to be in possession of the murder weapon?"

"The knife? I found it."

"Where did you find it?"

"On the lawn of Rebecca Carwell's house."

"And why had you gone to her house?"

"At her invitation. We had become friends. Originally, we had met at a magic show at the Downs—but Rebecca had invited me to her home many times. I liked the house and, from the first visit, intended to use it in the book."

"And on the day of her murder you happened to find a bloody knife lying on the lawn?"

"Well, yes."

"In the front yard."

"Yes."

"Dad, I just remembered something," Herculeah interrupted. "When Gilda—Miss Hayworth—and I were going up the walk, at a certain point she glanced over at the lawn and stumbled. I know, I just *know* she was remembering the day she threw the knife there, because she looked pale and I said—"

"I'd like to get on with my questioning, Herculeah, if you don't mind."

"But I felt that would be important. You see, if—"

"Herculeah."

"Yes, Dad."

Chico Jones sighed. "Now getting back to the knife. You saw it on the lawn?"

"Yes."

"And you picked it up?"

"After wrapping it carefully in my scarf."

"Why, Mr. King?"

"I thought it might turn out to be important. Also"—he gave a shrug—"I have a weakness for weapons. I cannot resist."

"After you wrapped the knife—carefully in your scarf—did you then proceed up the steps to the house?"

"I did."

"And?"

"I rang the bell, but no one came to the door."

"Did that seem strange to you?"

"Yes, but—"

"But what?"

"Nothing. I thought she had gone out and that I would call her that evening. I did call that evening, but got no answer."

"When did you learn of Miss Carwell's death?"

"I read about it in the paper."

"And did you not, upon reading it in the paper, think perhaps the knife was of importance?"

"I guess I didn't make the connection."

"Yes, he did, Dad," Herculeah said, "because he told me that there was blood on the knife and—"

"I'll handle this, Herculeah."

"Actually I think I did tell her that."

Chico Jones turned his eyes back to Mathias King. "You tampered with evidence and obstructed justice, Mr. King, and I'm going to see that you're charged."

"Should I call my lawyer?"

"I think you're going to need one. There may be additional charges after I speak with my daughter."

Chico Jones turned to the sergeant, who was closing his notebook. "You have anything else, Sergeant?"

"No, sir."

"Then I suggest we all go home. Herculeah, would you and Meat like a ride?"

"Yes." They said the word together as if it was old times.

Herculeah and Meat got in the backseat of the car and sat side by side.

"Oh, I've got so much to tell you, Meat. I don't know where to begin. I'll start at Death's Door."

She told about her visit with Uncle Neiman, then about her Tai Chi class, and then about the murder house.

When she got to the part about the tea party at One Kings Row, she happened to glance up and see that her father was watching her in the rearview mirror.

"Don't look at me like that."

"Like what?"

"Like I've done something criminal."

"Have you done something criminal?"

"Well, if you're planning on accusing me of illegal entry, it won't stick. I had an invitation. The only thing you can possibly accuse me of is breaking and exiting, which I did."

She turned back to Meat. "Now, where was I?" she said.

29

A FINAL QUESTION

"You won't believe who called me," Herculeah said to Meat. It was eleven o'clock, and she and Meat were having their evening phone conversation.

"Not the murderess."

"No, Mathias King. He wanted to apologize for everything that happened. He explained that he'd had writer's block, and he felt that if he could see me on the sacrificial altar, it would cure him."

"I'm still glad you didn't do it."

"Me, too, but you know what? He said he had been writing all evening. He said just seeing the sacrificial dagger pierce my chest did the trick. Course it didn't actually pierce my chest."

"It sure looked like it did."

"And you still can't believe I'm alive."

"That wasn't what I was going to say." Actually, it had been exactly what he was going to say, but he thought quickly and came up with: "So what do you think this had to do with Hercules? All of your other cases involved one of the labors of Hercules—the Cretan Bull, the Many-Headed Hydra."

"Well, remember when we were in Hidden Treasures and Mathias King was describing the murders in his book?"

"I remember."

"And remember he described a poison cup? The goblet was shaped like an apple?"

"I remember."

"So I immediately remembered the golden apples of the Hesperides."

"I hope you also remember him almost choking me to death with the golden noose. My throat still feels tight when I think of it."

"But now I know it wasn't that. I looked this up on the Internet to make sure; all of Hercules's labors were done for the king of Tiryns and Mycenae. His name was King Eurystheus. I hope I'm pronouncing that right."

"Sounds good to me."

Of course, just Herculeah's voice sounded good to him now.

"That king's labors almost did Hercules in, and our Mathias King almost did the same to me."

There was a silence. Meat was afraid Herculeah was going to hang up if he didn't say something soon, but she spoke first.

"Oh, there is something I wanted to ask you, Meat."

Meat's heart sank. Here it comes.

"What?"

"Well, I've pretty much figured out what happened with you last Saturday."

"You have?"

"Sure. Like I told my mom, I'm a detective. My talent is figuring things out. I just need you to fill in a blank or two. I figured out that your mom pressured you to go on the outing, with—" She paused for Meat to fill in the name.

"Steffie." He wished he had said Stephanie, but the damage was done now.

"And I don't know the name of the woman who asked your mom to arrange the outing." She still didn't like the word *date*.

"Dottie."

"And I don't know what movie you went to see—"

"*Teen Mutants.*"

"Or what kind of pizza you had."

"Pepperoni."

"Oh. And there's one other thing. You're the only person I know in the world who can answer this question."

"What? What's the question?"

"You probably won't want to tell me...."

"I'll tell you anything. What do you want to know? What?"

"Well, I can't get that book you mentioned off my mind. I want to know if, since Hee had the loud hee-haw, well, did it bother Haw that his hee-haw was softer? Would it be possible for him to go to a speech therapist for help with his hee-haw?"

Meat froze. Could Herculeah possibly know about his afternoon nightmare? Could she actually know he had brayed in her face? After all, she knew everything else.

"Have you already forgotten your famous author Elizabeth Ann Varner and Hee and Haw?"

And when she said that, Meat was infused with happiness. He realized that nothing she could have said would have made him happier.

This meant that things were back to normal. You didn't appreciate how good normal was until you experienced abnormal.

"I'll lend you the book."

"You have the book?"

"Yes, but it's an autographed copy, so you'll have to promise to take good care of it."

Herculeah laughed. "I never know when you're being serious and when you're putting me on."

"Good."

There was another silence. But this was a comfortable silence. Meat was sorry when Herculeah broke it.

"I've got to go. Mom's yelling at me. Will I see you tomorrow?"

"What do you think?"

"I hope so."

"Oh, you will. You always do."

"Then good night, Meat."

"Good night, Herculeah."